PRAISE FOR GRACE GREENE'S BOOKS

Love the beach and Coastal Carolina? Consider reading the two series set in Emerald Isle, NC because ~ *It's always a good time for a love story and a trip to the beach!*

THE EMERALD ISLE, NC STORIES SERIES begins with the award-winning debut novel, *Beach Rental*, an RT Book Reviews TOP PICK. Here's what the reviewer wrote:

> "No author can come close to capturing the awe-inspiring essence of the North Carolina coast like Greene. Her debut novel seamlessly combines hope, love and faith, like the female equivalent of Nicholas Sparks. Her writing is meticulous and so finely detailed you'll hear the gulls overhead and the waves crashing onto shore. Grab a hanky, bury your toes in the sand and get ready to be swept away with this unforgettable beach read."

Or visit Emerald Isle, NC in the BAREFOOT TIDES SERIES that begins with *A Barefoot Tide*, in which a woman from the rural town of Cub Creek, Virginia accepts a temporary job that takes her to the beach—and discovers it may not be so easy to go home again.

Regarding Cub Creek, Virginia—a rural area *in the heart of Virginia, where the forests hide secrets and the creeks run strong and deep*—where Libbie (in *Cub Creek*) goes to hide from a world where she doesn't fit in…and finds her life. Or where Hannah (in *The Memory of Butterflies*) keeps a devastating secret to protect her loved ones. Or where Kara (in *Wildflower Heart*) finds healing from old wounds and heartbreak. Or where Jaynie (in *A Light Last Seen*) finds that you can—and often *should*—go home again.

A Light Last Seen and A Reader's View of Cub Creek

From a reader about Cub Creek and A Light Last Seen: "'In the heart of Virginia, where the forests hide secrets and the creeks run strong and deep,' is a place called Cub Creek. A place that has meadows filled with colorful flowers and butterflies to chase, and dirt roads and Cub Creek to jump over and disappear into the woods. A living and rural place that draws the reader to the setting and the characters who have stories to tell. A place with light and darkness and as unique as the characters who live there. When I opened the beautiful cover of this book, I stepped into the Cub Creek world and met the main character, Jaynie Highsmith. This is her story."—*Reader/Reviewer Bambi Rathman, February 2020*

A Crimson Heart

A Crimson Heart

A Thanksgiving and Christmas Novella

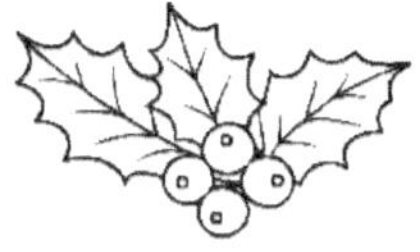

By Grace Greene

Kersey Creek Books

Acknowledgments

My sincere thanks to everyone who contributed to making *A Crimson Heart* the best story it could be, especially Kellie Coates Gilbert who offered her time and feedback to make this a better book, and to my editor, Jessica Fogleman who has edited so many of my books that I can't imagine releasing a new story without the assurance of her keen eye and magic touch.

Dedication

A Crimson Heart is dedicated to caregivers
and to those who receive the care.
Both sides of that action are blessed.

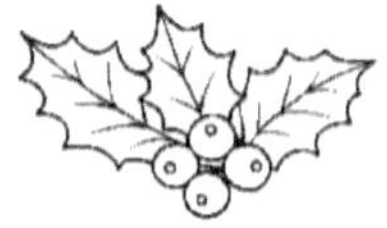

And now, faith, hope, love, abide these three;
but the greatest of these is love.
1 Corinthians 13:13 (NKJV)

A CRIMSON HEART

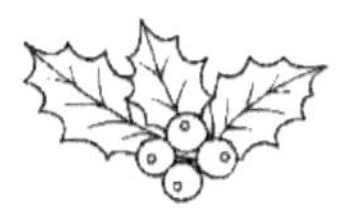

Prologue

Red is the color of love and sometimes of romance. It is the color of cranberries and poinsettias and Santa's suit. Red is the color of the blooms on Mary Hennipen's once-prized camellia bushes—now seriously overgrown—and of the bumper crop of berries on the holly trees. It is also the color of the knitted scarf I wound about my neck this morning before setting out on this chilly November day in Virginia in the foothills of the Blue Ridge Mountains.

The forest path that leads from my small home to Hennipen House is good for walking. It's especially pleasant in warmer weather, but even in winter the walk is peaceful. Thus, this morning when I received an early call from Megan notifying me that she'd be late, I set out on foot for Hennipen House.

Aunt Henny can be left on her own for short periods

of time, but we are all more comfortable when someone is with her. I think she is too.

In this area where the Hennipen backyard meets the forest, there's a half-hidden corner of the woods with a bench surrounded by mature camellias, hollies, and rhododendrons, all very old and thus huge. This used to be a beautiful, well-tended garden. Now the chipped, discolored birdbath is overwhelmed by spreading branches, but its bowl still catches water when the rain falls, and some days I sit on the bench and watch the birds and other small critters go about their business—but not today. Today, I pause only to stare at the branches of a small tree that has grown uninvited in the midst of the evergreen bushes.

This skinny sapling sprang up a few years back and is already several inches taller than I. It is bare of leaves this time of year, as it should be, but it's an unexpected sight with small red ribbons tied to its branches.

With a sigh, I reach into my coat pocket and pull out a new ribbon, pressing its silkiness gently to my lips before securing it in a bow among its fellows.

Done, I turn away because—as Robert Frost so beautifully wrote—*the woods are lovely, dark and deep, but I have promises to keep.*

Promises. Humph. Well, someone has to keep them, don't they? Even when those promises are not ours and that duty shouldn't fall on us.

Before me, the roof turrets and shingled peaks of Hennipen House are visible, appearing in the gaps between the treetops, much like magical promises.

There is no magic here now, if there ever was.

The mass of trees disguises the reality—a sad truth of time and decay and broken toys—of the impossibility of holding back time, even one's own personal timeline.

Same with people too. You can't force them to stay with you when they decide to move on.

We haven't had snow yet this season. When it snows, the cold white blanket will change this landscape, giving it an element of mystery, of beauty, concealing the everyday truth of neglect. It will be an untainted landscape of potential. It will be like the day Simon first told me he loved me. We were seated right here on this bench, and again, a year later, when he proposed.

I hear a noise in the brush and turn abruptly to scan the trees. A cardinal, bright red—as red as the camellia blossoms and the holly berries—lands on the birdbath. A male. He cocks his head to the side as he notices me. He gives me a long look as if surprised to see me here . . . or maybe surprised to see anyone out here at all in the cold, in a place where so few come now. After a stare, he bobs his head and flies off.

Just a bird.

I'm watching him disappear into the cedars and pine trees when I hear a voice calling in the distance. A sudden gust of wind carries the sound to me, and I listen, my breath held, because the voice seems . . . *No, not familiar.* I haven't heard *his* voice in years.

But in the next second, I know I am both wrong and right, because I *do* know this voice, and there is nothing ethereal going on here. In a flash, I'm running past the last of the trees, over the small bridge where the creek flows and toward the turrets and peaks.

Chapter One

The Hennipen family of Crimson Grove had been quite the thing in years past. But times had changed—*as time does*. The last several generations of Hennipens had sold off acreage, little by little, to pay their bills. Aunt Henny used to say the decline started during the Great Depression back in the 1930s. Likely that was true. But the decline was a slow one and probably was tied more to the economic health of Crimson Grove itself which has had its own ups and downs over the past century.

Not too distant from the Hennipen property, the town's main street had been eclipsed by modern economic growth, though the shops on Main had assumed a quaint quality and were surviving pretty well, unlike Hennipen House, which had become much like a landlocked island of forest and house. We were surrounded by subdivisions and strip malls that had grown up all around us like—well, like *weeds*—per Aunt Henny.

Named Mary by her mother, someone had called her Henny (short for Hennipen) when she was a kid, and the nickname had stuck. She'd been born a Hennipen and had married a distant Hennipen cousin and the happy couple had hoped to produce many more Hennipens to carry on the family name. They'd succeeded with Simon's father,

Thomas, who had, in turn, sired Simon. Henny's only other child was Lisa. She'd married and had taken her husband's name, Harper, and now she was a widow, too. Lisa's two daughters were off somewhere. I had no idea where. We hadn't seen them in years. And that had been it as far as offspring went.

It seemed to me that measuring a family's present and future health by focusing on a particular surname was bound to fail sooner or later, but no one had asked my opinion.

As for me, Henny wasn't my actual aunt. That was only a courtesy title.

So, Aunt Henny was the last of the Hennipen line—at least here in this town—because Lisa was ill and stuck in Florida. Henny's grandson, Simon, whom she'd raised, was gone. And me? I lived on the far side of the forest, yes, but still in Crimson Grove, which somehow meant I could be here more often than I *should* because, through some convoluted familial and generational ties of friendship and circumstance, she'd become my problem.

Past the trees and bushes, I had a clear view of the house. And yes, there was Aunt Henny standing on the back porch. Another gust of wind caused her to sway as it pressed her frayed housecoat against her thin frame. Her arms were bare. Her legs were bare. Those worn slippers on her feet were going to trip her up when she reached the concrete steps. I ran.

"Stop, Henny. Wait!"

I caught up to her, putting my hands on her arms. "It's cold out here. Let's get in the house."

She resisted. "That boy, he came back again." She glanced beyond me, back toward the garden, insisting, "I saw him. I came out here to give him a piece of my mind."

I put my arm around her to shift her direction back toward the house and felt her trembling. I said gently, "I heard you calling me."

She pushed at me. "Not you." With her free hand, she gestured, jabbing her index finger in the direction of the forest. "That boy."

"You're shivering. You'll catch your death out here . . . plus, *I'm* freezing." I gave an exaggerated shiver. "Let's go inside now."

This time she cooperated, and soon we were back in the house. I grabbed the sofa blanket and draped it around her to warm her up.

"Aunt Henny, you can't be going out like that." I ditched my jacket and went to heat water for tea.

"Don't tell me what I can or can't do."

"It's winter. If you don't have sense enough to put on a coat or wear proper shoes—"

She interrupted, saying, "Don't lecture me. I'll do as I must."

That gave me pause. Gently, I said, "Tell me what you *must do*, and I'll help you."

She made a rude noise. "That boy—"

"There was no boy. I was out there alone, on my way here."

"He pulls the flowers off my camellias. He tears them off and steals them." She shook her head. "I won't have it."

"Aunt Henny, honey, there's no boy."

She closed her expression, pressing her lips together and shutting her eyes as she turned her face away.

I closed my eyes too and sighed. I found it hard to be patient and intuitive and all that good stuff. I wasn't that person, and this wasn't supposed to be my responsibility.

Scooting a chair close to her, I sat knee to knee with her. Her bone-thin hands were clenched in her lap. I put mine over them. "Let it go, Henny. If you see the boy again, tell me right away. I'll run out there and talk to him."

Her eyes opened slowly, the look in them unexpectedly keen. She said, "You won't. You don't even believe me."

I gasped. What could I say? The truth? *Okay.*

"You are right, Henny. It's been many years since I've seen a boy, or anyone else except Stu, in your backyard, and I'm not sure this boy truly exists. I think you glimpsed me out there today, half hidden by the trees and . . ." I squeezed her hands gently. "I promise you that if you see him again, tell me. I'll be out there in a heartbeat to investigate."

"You'll tell that boy to stop pulling the blooms off my camellias?"

"I promise." I shook my head. "But why do you care if . . . if there's a child out there who wants a few flowers? Flowers don't last, anyway."

She squeezed my hands this time. "This is when they bloom. When everything else is sleeping in winter, that's when those camellias thrive and look their best. They deserve their time to shine without being ripped away from where they belong."

I nodded. "Indeed they do, Henny." I smiled and tried to hide the sadness that surely showed on my face. The grief of it all. This was important to her in *this* moment. But it wouldn't last. The shining times for her were brief now. Soon her brain would reset. That was the real sadness. She'd forget this obsession with the imaginary boy and her camellia bushes. Such a reset might be sad, but it was also a kindness.

They said—*they* being the doctors—that she was in the early stages of dementia. Of course, they hadn't said it to *me*. They'd told Henny's daughter, Lisa, who'd passed the info to my mother, who'd then relayed the information to me. Truly annoying.

Lisa and I had never gotten along.

Yet with the help of daily caregivers, including one who stayed overnight, Henny was able to live at home, as she wished. When those caregivers faltered or had unexpected illnesses or such, somehow I'd become the backup. Lisa had no objection to that. And because I had a family connection, the other caregivers assumed I was in charge.

Another truth was that Henny seemed worse lately, more volatile and irrational. It worried me.

I was feeling inadequate and hoping I was doing the right thing by helping her . . . and about as confident and self-determining as this old house.

"Don't slouch, Amelia," Henny said.

I straightened my spine and sat taller. I held my head

high and smiled at her.

One thing Henny and I had in common? We might feel put upon from time to time, and we might even grouse and complain, but we weren't victims. Henny and I . . . I nodded for my own benefit. We weren't pushovers. Not for long. Sometimes it just took us a bit to get our feet firmly under us and figure out how and when to make a stand or take action.

CঙঠৎO

Henny napped in her recliner while I washed up our lunch dishes. I was thinking about the boy. *The one who doesn't exist,* I reminded myself. I felt guilty as I stared through the window at the old garden. Henny must've caught sight of me through the foliage. From this vantage point, I saw how the small tree with its ribbons blended with the evergreen bushes behind and beside it. The spots of red that peeked through the few trees, now bare, looked a lot like tiny flowers. She might've seen me adding the new ribbon and misunderstood.

The camellias had bloomed with gusto in late October, and should still be blooming, but for whatever reason the red blossoms with their golden centers had all but ceased. We were well into November now, and I doubted Henny could see the few remaining blooms from the house. Mistaking me out there for a boy messing with her bushes had just been one small step farther along the road of her imaginings.

Aunt Henny had always been known for her flights of fancy. We'd had that in common too, though I'd lost my wings years ago. Maybe she'd *found* hers again.

So, though not intentional, Henny's distress was my fault. Her imagination had taken the bits and pieces from what she'd seen and had flown into unexpected territory.

Speaking of flights of fancy, it didn't take much imagination to understand how the miscreant happened to be a boy with dark, glossy curls. In Henny's mind, he probably had a smile much like Simon's . . . mischievous. One that could melt a grandmother's heart. And mine too.

Henny had raised her grandson after his parents died. She had adored him.

I sighed. Along with the dark hair, had she given the boy Simon's eyes? Those steely gray . . .

If she could see her grandson in this boy, imaginary or not, I wondered how she saw this *property*, her home? As it had been many years ago? Surely not as I and others saw it.

The present reality of Hennipen House was obvious outside each time I crossed the little arched bridge over a creek that was hardly more than a meager, weed-choked stream now. But the front of the house . . . For whatever reason, the decay there bothered me even more. I preferred the forest path.

Every week or two—or three—Stu Perkins hauled his riding mower over, towing it on a trailer behind his pickup. Stu cut the grass and other greenery to discourage snakes and ticks and insects. *I don't trim,* he'd said.

Each visit, Stu planted his butt on the seat of the

mower. Anything the machine could run over was fair game. If the machine couldn't . . . well, then the greenery thrived, as it did along the creek bank and around the remains of the old sandbox. What bothered me the most was how the grass clumped, growing high and thick around the legs of the rusted, listing swing set—including the seat that dangled by one rusted chain—because *Stu didn't trim*. Or *move stuff out of the way*.

But Stu did *work for cheap*, and since Lisa controlled Henny's funds and her medical care from afar, she was the one who made such decisions. I reminded myself that Stu might not be as particular about his lawncare efforts as I would like, but in this case, something was better than nothing.

⊂Ⴒ℘⊃

Henny lived in three rooms—the TV room, a first-floor bedroom, and the kitchen. This huge house, beyond those three rooms, was like a mausoleum. Or perhaps a museum piece, fully furnished with what were now antiques. The doors were kept shut to help lower the heating and cooling bills. Every so often, I walked the house and opened each door, checking for water leaks and whatever other indignity age might be inflicting on this place. In the unlikely event someone might come to call, I kept the front room tidy and dusted—the parlor, as the family had always called it.

Henny ignored my efforts, and Lisa never asked about

the state of the house.

Since Henny was still napping, I grabbed a dustcloth and a dry mop. I pushed aside the massive pocket doors and left the doorway open onto the foyer so I'd hear Henny if she woke.

Quickly and efficiently, I worked my way around the room. I always finished in the same spot, at the drop-leaf table on which Henny had—in better days—squeezed in as many framed photographs as she could possibly fit. I picked up the photograph of Simon and me.

The photo had been taken on our wedding day. My mom and dad, Aunt Henny, Lisa and her husband, and, of course, Simon and me—we were all posed, arm in arm and smiling, on the front steps of this very house, where we'd just held the wedding and reception.

My dad had passed soon after. Lisa was now seriously ill with cancer, and her chemo treatments were taking a toll on her. She couldn't have helped her mother even if she'd been here, locally. Mom was right about that.

I examined those dear faces from years before. Our fates had been decided with all the care one might find in a metaphorical game of musical chairs. Life's music had played, and when the music stopped, we'd each grabbed for the nearest chairs. Dad had been the odd man out, soon to leave us. I missed him even after all these years. As for Simon and me, we'd found ourselves in the same chair. We'd tried to share it, but the joke was on us. Simon had been sincere in his promise to *love and cherish* me *in sickness and in health, until death us do part*—I believed that. He *had* loved me. But after a few years, he'd simply decided marriage wasn't for him.

He'd told me that ever so politely on his way out the door.

After a lifetime of friendship (till that point), two years of dating, and five years of marriage, politeness didn't make it hurt any less.

As for the rest of the players? Lisa and her husband had departed for the sunnier climes of Florida, as had my mother. Only Henny and I remained in that imaginary, now empty room, where the music had stopped and had never resumed playing.

And that photo of Simon and me? In its carved mahogany frame with inset gold hearts? It felt wrong. As if it represented something that was still true—but wasn't. Like a lie.

I put the wedding photo back. I would've turned it face down, if there'd been room on the tabletop.

My heart ached as I picked up the photo of Simon as a boy. It showed a dark-haired child standing in front of the camellias that formed a backdrop of lush green leaves and crimson blooms in happier times.

Mine wasn't the only heart that had been broken when Simon left me. And that wasn't anyone's imagination. It was a simple truth.

Aunt Henny would soon forget the imaginary boy. She'd have a memory reset. That's what I told myself, feeling too de-energized to consider the matter further. Tomorrow, Henny wouldn't even remember she'd seen a kid in the garden. She'd go back to thinking of Simon—when she thought of him—as being on an extended trip.

I'd told her the truth once about her beloved grandson's departure and even that he wasn't coming home, and why, but she'd chosen to forget the unwelcome news. If that was how she wanted it, I could go along with that. Maybe she found comfort in ignoring reality.

Megan arrived midafternoon. She was petite and energetic and kind. Her dark ponytail bounced when she walked. Henny liked her, so that was good.

"Sorry," Megan said. "My car wouldn't start. Had to get a new battery."

She waved off my *"Don't worry about it"* as she moved the wet laundry into the dryer.

"I'm just glad it happened now, 'cause winter's coming. Cold's hard on batteries. Don't want to be stranded somewhere with a dead one."

She punched the start button, and the dryer went into action. She gave me a long look.

"The bad news is that I have a dentist appointment in the morning. Not sure if you remember?"

No, I hadn't remembered. "No problem, I'll come over."

"Heaven knows what Miss Henny will do if you ever get a job."

I shrugged. "That will be her daughter's problem."

Megan said, "She's still real sick, right?"

"Yes."

"Well, they're lucky to have you taking care of things up here."

I answered, "I think we're very fortunate to have you and Bianca, and the others who help out."

Megan nodded. She'd taken a clean towel from the drawer and was giving the dishes in the drainer a once-over to ensure they were dry before they went into the cabinet.

"That's true." She paused, then added, "Hey, I noticed you dusted the front room again. Want me to take it on? I don't mind. The whole house, and everything in it, would be too big a chore for me, but one room, I can handle."

"Not necessary. I'm the only one who cares anyway."

"Oh, she cares. Yes, ma'am. Ms. Henny doesn't say it. Doesn't like to admit it. But I can tell."

I shook my head. "I don't think she ever goes into the parlor, or any of the other rooms."

"Well, yes and no. She thinks about it, but she says they're too full of ghosts. Memory-type ghosts, if you know what I mean. No *actual* ghosts—she doesn't want to see *that*, for sure." She smiled. "But she notices, believe you me." She muttered something as she put away the dry dishes, then said louder, "Every so often, she has me push open those parlor doors. She just stands there, never going in, then has me shut them again." She laughed. "Like pushing trucks up Maple Street, aren't they? Those doors weigh a ton."

"Yeah, I do know what you mean." And I did. Especially about the memories . . . maybe not the *actual* memories, but the memory of the expectations she'd had in the good days when she *thought* she knew what her latter years would look like.

Henny didn't want to face the memories of hopes that never came true, and I couldn't fault her for that.

Chapter Two

I was expecting Aunt Henny to have an overnight memory reset, but I was wrong.

Megan had her dental appointment that morning, and I needed to make a trip to the grocery store later, so when I headed for Hennipen House, I drove.

I steeled myself not to flinch at the sight of the house and property from the front. It always seemed to me that the deterioration was most pronounced there, and terribly visible to anyone who came to the house.

The longish driveway between the house and Maple Street used to be gracious, but now the asphalt was cracked and sunken in spots. Seeing the house from the front . . .

The dismay, even that vague sense of guilt I felt at the crooked shutters, the peeling paint on the doorframe, the pitted concrete of the wide front steps . . . Why?

It was the pesky logic of time again. But was it the fault of time? Or merely evidence of a family either past caring or too cash-strapped to keep up what generations of a family once thought important? Especially if that generation was down to one old woman who was too stubborn to allow time itself to move on.

As soon as I walked into the house, what did I hear? *Henny.*

Her world had not reset itself overnight. In fact, if anything, she was worse and more determined.

She was in the kitchen, standing at the window again, her fingers leaving marks all over the glass, as she stared outside and complained loudly. I saw it in her tense posture, I saw it in the slide of her hands down the panes of glass, but at least she wasn't shouting or trying to run outside.

With a warning look, Bianca said, "She slept fine last night. But as soon as she was up and out of bed, she started in at that window."

Henny was still in her nightgown.

"Did she eat breakfast yet?"

"Nope. Sorry. I've been trying to calm her down. The oatmeal's in the pan on the stove. Want me to try again?"

"I've got it." I grinned rather grimly. "Thanks, Bianca. Thank you for your patience and for hanging in, especially on the rough days."

Throughout our conversation, Henny showed no signs of hearing us, not even acknowledging my arrival or Bianca's departure. She'd switched from fussing over boys and her camellias to going on about *important things.* About how there were important things missing, things that she needed to find. She was roaming the rooms and angsting over it and searching in a wholly ineffectual way. I tried to distract and divert. I'd learned that was the best way to deal with her in this mood.

Frankly, trying to sort out the real from the imaginary problems was exhausting.

And Megan wouldn't arrive until sometime after noon.

How long could this last? I didn't know.

As I checked the pot of oatmeal—it was still warm—I told myself I should get a real job. Then I could tell Mom and Lisa that I couldn't help Henny every day because *I HAD A JOB*. Those words felt like all caps even as a thought. And a lie. Because these days I had no impetus or drive to do anything, including job-hunting. Henny needed me. Maybe when Lisa was better . . . But who was I kidding? Lisa, even if she recovered her health, had no intention whatsoever of returning to Crimson Grove for more than as short a stay as she could get away with.

"Aunt Henny," I said softly, hoping not to startle her, but merely to distract her and switch her focus. "Aunt Henny," I repeated, louder this time. "What are you doing? What's up?"

She said, without turning around, "You know." She muttered a few syllables more under her breath, then continued, "You know *exactly what's up*."

I said, "Oh?"

"You said you'd take care of it."

I said . . . what? When?

She added, "He's after my flowers again."

"You mean the camellia bushes?"

But she was annoyed and I was there, so she threw back at me, "What other flowers have I got this time of year? You know I haven't put in winter pansies in years."

"Aunt Henny, let me see." I moved to stand right behind her this time, thinking maybe the closeness would comfort her.

I put my hands gently on her shoulders and spoke calmly. "You stay inside where it's warm, and I'll step out there and take a look. How about that? You promise to stay here at this window? *Right here*, where I can look back and see you. Don't wander off, okay?"

"Don't you worry about me." As if to emphasize that, she continued staring straight ahead.

"I'll be quick. Stand here."

I hurried because her focus was iffy at best. She couldn't be counted on to follow through with her promise. But I knew she was also watching me as I ran across the yard because I felt her eyes on my back.

Past the old sandbox and the decrepit swing set, I made a show of standing where the woods began and looking around. I was turning this way and that and finished the show by raising my arms in a big shrug to indicate no one was out here in the garden—and something caught my eye.

A small red bow was lying on the grass near the creek bridge.

I scanned the woods around me. A squirrel chittered up on a branch, probably annoyed that I was intruding. A squirrel or even one of the larger birds could've nabbed that bright ribbon and dropped it there. If I climbed the trees or checked out the burrows, I'd probably find one or more of them had been gaily decorated in red satin. That amused me. The woodland creatures were preparing for the holidays to come—obviously even the Hennipen *squirrels* were special.

I'd already been gone long enough for Henny to have gotten into trouble. I hurried back across the yard and found her still in the kitchen, but not at the window. She was seated at the kitchen table. Waiting. She seemed anxious, her eyes big as she watched me.

"No one, dear Henny. Only a squirrel." I tried to lighten her mood with a joke. "I think that squirrel was decorating his nest." I placed the ribbon on the table beside her, wondering what she'd make of it.

"Decorating?" Her eyes focused on the ribbon.

"The holidays are almost here. Thanksgiving. Christmas." Even as I said the words, I feared I'd regret it. Last year . . . it had been grim.

She grunted.

Gently, I said, "After Megan gets here this afternoon, I'll ask around the neighborhood about small dark-haired boys."

She looked away.

I added, "If I find him, I'll speak gently to him. Help him understand why it's wrong to take the blossoms." I patted her hand. "Now for breakfast. Let me fix your oatmeal, and after you eat, we'll get you ready for the day."

She looked downcast.

I leaned down so that I could look back up at her bowed head and catch her eyes. With a teasing smile, I said, "You can't go around in your nightgown all day, you know. Besides, I have my car. We can take a ride out about town like we used to do. Remember when?"

With that, she returned my smile, almost shyly.

At some point while I was getting breakfast on the table, the ribbon disappeared. Henny ate well and seemed quietly, almost smugly pleased about something. During the breakfast cleanup, I checked under the table and in the trash can. No red ribbon.

My dear Henny.

The ride went well, but as we drove down Main Street, she got quieter and quieter, staring fiercely out the car window. I didn't know what was going on in her head, for sure. I suspected her mood had something to do with the garland strung overhead from one side of the street to the other and the glitter and holly adorning the storefronts.

I hadn't been in town recently. Stupidly, it hadn't occurred to me that the decorations would already be up.

During lunch, she was still subdued and vague, as if her mind was elsewhere. I let her be. If she wanted conversation, she'd tell me. Doubtless, she was tired. But instinct told me there was more to it.

I tidied the kitchen and ran a load of clothing in the washer while Henny dozed in front of a television game show in the den. When Megan arrived, we exchanged notes, and I left.

I sat in my car in front of the house for a few minutes, thinking.

Aunt Henny might forget my promise, right? But would she? She'd remembered us discussing it the day before. She might remember again tomorrow. Keeping promises still meant something . . . to some people.

I'd ask around, that's what I told her. About small dark-haired boys.

But by the time I'd driven down Henny's driveway all the way to Maple Street and stopped . . . I hesitated, keeping my foot on the brake.

I'd ask around. But where?

I shifted the car into park and turned the engine off before opening the door wide. I was blocking the driveway, but who'd care? No one.

Stepping out onto the broken asphalt, I looked both ways along Maple Street. That subdivision—many acres all once owned by the Hennipen family—I knew no one—not a single soul—who lived here now. Those houses, small and showing their years . . . I'd never knocked on a door in this neighborhood, not even once. Was I going to do that now? To ask strangers about a boy?

How crazy would that sound?

A blue car drove past. A woman was driving. She glanced my way and kept going.

I sighed. There was no sidewalk, just a narrow dirt-and-rock verge between the road and a ditch. Once upon a time, I must've walked down this road, but it would have been ages ago. I strolled slowly along now, my hands in my coat pockets. It was chilly, and overhead the dark clouds hung low. I wouldn't go far. Just a short distance. Maybe inspiration would strike.

Maple Street had a heavy aura that aligned with the mostly denuded trees, their branches stark and grasping against a cloudy sky. Only a few leaves were still clinging, forgotten until Mother Nature was in the mood to come back in force and claim the stragglers. The houses here had only a narrow space between them. The buildings were aging, and the lawns had the usual dry dullness that comes as autumn creeps closer to winter.

I shivered. A drop of wet touched my face. I looked up and waited to see if another drop would follow and asked myself if it wouldn't be smarter to turn around and hotfoot it back to my car, when a horn sounded. I nearly jumped out of my skin and pivoted to face it.

A truck—a large pickup. I hadn't even heard it coming. I'd been standing in the road, staring up at the clouds. Now I was staring at a truck. Through the windshield, I watched as the driver lifted his hand from the steering wheel in a half wave.

Could a wave convey annoyance? Maybe mockery?

I raised my own hand in acknowledgment and apology and stepped aside to stand on the side of the road. He drove forward slowly and stopped, rolling his window down.

"Are you okay, ma'am?"

"Pardon?"

He asked, "Need help?"

He looked a little rough, a large man with his arm resting on the open window of his truck, but his voice was low, with a warm quality. My brain made an irrational leap—that somehow his voice indicated he was a reasonable person. Maybe the eyes showed that too. They were a deep brown, with tiny flecks of a lighter color.

I said, "Sorry I was blocking the road. Thanks for

not running over me."

Pointing above, he said, "You're about to get rained on. Need a ride?"

I shook my head. "Thanks, but I'm good."

"Take care, then," he said. "Best advice? Don't daydream in the middle of the road."

He drove away. Had he been smiling when he said that about not daydreaming in the road?

Nope. Not smiling. Though there'd been a certain light in his eyes that indicated amusement at my expense.

No blame to him—I'd earned that *advice*. On the other hand, if I'd provided someone, anyone, with a laugh—even a silent, derisive one—it was okay. My ego could withstand it.

I headed back to my car, acknowledging that I wasn't going to knock on any doors seeking a boy with dark curls. If he did in truth exist, and if he wanted to help himself to the red ribbons . . . fine with me. I'd bought them in bulk and had a ton yet to hang.

Aunt Henny might feel differently, but I'd deal with it or circumvent it.

Climbing back into my car, I closed the door and restarted the car.

Time to go home, by way of the grocery store, then to return to my humble but peaceful cottage where I only had to worry about myself. It was the only refuge I had, and I was feeling in great need of a retreat.

Chapter Three

The next morning, I walked over to Henny's house. I had almost reached her back porch when my cell phone rang. I glanced at the screen. *Mom.*

I stopped to answer. "Hey there. What's up?"

"Amelia, where are you?"

"Almost at Henny's back door." Yes, there was sarcasm in my tone. I'd had a quick phone chat with mom just before leaving the house and she knew—

She interrupted, saying, "Hurry, Amelia. It might already be too late."

"What?" I rushed up the steps. The back screened door was latched, but I reached through a gash in the screening to twist the knob of the kitchen door. The knob turned, but the door wouldn't budge.

The slide bolt at the top of the door must have been secured. We used that on days when Henny was prone to wander. Through the glass, I saw lights were on, but no one was in sight.

"I have to run around to the front, Mom. Hold on."

I ran, my pack jouncing on my back. As I raced around the house and turned the corner, Mom was saying, "Megan called Lisa. Said she tried to call you. She told Lisa that Henny was agitated and fell and hit her head."

"Hold on, Mom. I see them. I'll call you back."

The ambulance was what I saw first; next was Henny strapped to a gurney with two EMS techs walking it down the sidewalk. A third uniformed person, a woman, was speaking to Meg. I hurried over to them.

Meg saw me coming and called out, "She fell. Hit her head. They're taking her to the hospital."

"Is it serious?" *Silly question.* "How serious?"

"Falling and hitting her head . . . it has to be checked, regardless. I think she was unconscious but only briefly. She's a bit confused . . . but then, you know how she is, so it's hard to tell. Better to be safe. Get her looked at."

"Better to be safe, yes," I echoed. "I don't have my car. I walked over."

"I'll go with her. I'll follow the ambulance and give you a call when I know more." Her eyes opened wider. "I left some things cooking on the stove."

"No worries. I'll check."

The tech broke in, asking me, "Are you family?"

"No." I almost said, *Sort of,* before I added, "Her daughter is in Florida."

"Do you have a number for her?"

Megan said, "I've got it. I already called her daughter. We'd better go."

And they went. I watched them drive to the main road and vanish from sight.

Remembering what Megan had said, I hurried up the steps to the porch. I paused once more to look to that point where I'd last seen the ambulance.

As if this might be the last time.

I had a moment in which I held my breath, but then I released it in a sigh—one of relief. No, the Henny I knew, had known all my life, was one tough gal. A bump on the head might slow her down, but no more than that.

Henny would miss lunch, but she'd probably be back home in time for supper. To that end, I went inside to see what Megan had left on the stove.

⌘

I called Megan's number. I knew phone coverage in the hospital would be iffy, so I kept trying every so often. Finally, we connected.

"I was just about to drive on over. I was worried."

"You know how it is in the hospital. Hurry up and wait, right?" She sighed. "They are keeping her overnight." She hurried to add, "The scans look good, as I understand from Lisa. The doctors say that they want to keep her over as a precaution. If nothing goes awry, she'll come home tomorrow."

"How's Henny behaving?"

"Well, you know . . . But they're checking her for a UTI. Those can play havoc with the elderly." When I didn't speak, she continued, "If that's the cause for her recent . . . upsets . . . then treatment will help."

"It won't fix the dementia."

"No." Megan sighed. "I have to leave. I'm sorry I can't stay at the hospital with her."

"I appreciate all that you've done and are doing." And I did appreciate it. Without Megan and Bianca . . . payment was the least of it. The dedicated help they provided was hard to find. "I'll come to the hospital. I packed a small bag for Henny, just in case. I'll drive over. Will she be okay until I get there? Tell her not to worry, that I'm on my way."

"She's resting quietly now, but she isn't really alone. She's near the nurses' station. They're keeping a close eye on her."

"Okay then. Thank you again, and go home. Get some rest and enjoy your family."

I donned my scarf and fastened my coat, then picked up the small overnight bag of toiletries I'd packed for both Henny and me, just in case, and then hurried out to my car.

ʘʘ

I drove to the hospital, wondering how late I'd have to stay. Would they need me to stay overnight with her? I wasn't her medical power of attorney. I'd been nagging her daughter to get me listed as a contact for Henny, one to share medical info with. At any rate, there was no one in this area who was more closely connected to her than I, regardless of blood or legal ties. It was an impossible situation in so many ways.

A heart that was drivmen by obligation, legitimate or not, was heavy. However hard you tried to paste a smile on your face, still your feet dragged and your eyes refused to brighten.

I entered the hospital, seeking first the elevator and then walking down the hallway, checking the numbers on each room until I found the one I sought. The door was partway open. I listened, and hearing nothing, I pushed it wider and glanced in.

Henny was in bed, lying still and quiet. Her eyes were closed. I stood at the side of her bed and saw the large bruise that had formed from the bump on her forehead and had stained that side of her face, including halfway around her eye and down almost to her jaw.

It hurt to look at. But it probably didn't hurt her. That's how it had been with Henny's previous falls.

I sat on the vinyl-covered chair near her bed. I needed to speak with her when she woke, so that I could report back to Mom and Lisa, but truly, I didn't want to wake her. I didn't know what to say to her.

I laid my head back against the chair, feeling exhausted with . . . whatever. Resentment? Frustration?

"Amelia. Are you napping?"

Her hoarse voice startled me. I said, "You're awake."

She snorted, her usual response to obvious statements. "More importantly, get me out of here."

"Not yet. Not tonight. Probably tomorrow."

Agitated, she slapped the railing on the side of the bed with a clenched fist. "I have to get home."

"Why? It's not just the head injury, Henny. Apparently, you have a urinary tract infection. The doctor said you've probably been feeling pretty rough?"

She fixed her eyes on me.

"Between the head injury and the UTI, they want to keep you tonight to get all the good meds into you and make you better."

"Better," she said with a sigh, and her fist slipped gently from the railing and settled on the white blanket that covered her.

A small flush warmed me. *Better* would be good for all of us.

"You'll stay over, won't you?" she asked in a small voice.

In fact, she seemed to have shrunk, her body frail under that smooth white blanket, her legs so thin you could hardly tell they were under there.

"I don't know if the nurses will let me stay here tonight."

"No." She waved her hand. "At the house."

"At *your* house? Why? It's locked up tight. I made sure."

She waved both hands. "Someone will break in. They'll know I'm not there. Like that boy, maybe. Trespassers and others."

She'd become so agitated that I moved to stand beside her, caught her flailing hand in my own, holding it carefully. "It's all good, Henny. The house will be fine. I'll leave a couple of lamps burning."

"That won't fool anyone. They'll know. *It's my home.*"

It was the quivering lower lip that got me.

"Don't worry. I'll watch the house."

"All night?"

"All night."

I'd noticed the fist she was keeping close to her body. I touched it, asking, "Is your hand hurt? Maybe you hit that railing too hard?" I was actually concerned that it might indicate a stroke or such. I wasn't an expert.

"No, it's fine. I'm fine. Watch my house."

I nodded. "I will. I promise. But I can only do that if you work with the nurses and do as they say. If you don't, I'll have to leave the house empty and come back over here."

Her look went from mulish to accepting. We said goodbye and I gave her a light, quick kiss on her forehead, avoiding the bruised area.

I stopped at the nurses' desk to double-check with them instead of just leaving. I asked them to call me if she needed me during the night. The nurse said she'd let the others know. When I didn't walk away, she asked if there was something else she could help me with.

"Yes, actually. She's keeping one hand clenched tightly. She won't let me get a look at it. Do you know if she was injured, or could it be something more serious?"

The nurse smiled. "She's a stubborn one, isn't she? No, she came in with something in her hand and fussed like crazy when they tried to take it from her in the emergency room, and again when they brought her up here. We decided to let her keep it."

I waited, stunned.

The nurse gave a soft laugh and shook her head. "It's just a bit of red ribbon. A small bow." She paused, then added, "It seems to give her comfort."

I left.

Henny was stubborn indeed. She'd taken that ribbon and kept it with her through emergency medical techs, transport to the hospital, the emergency room treatment, and was still holding it as if it were a lifeline.

And me? I'd committed to an overnight stay at Hennipen House. During all the years I'd been in and out of that house, and even when Simon and I had lived there with Henny, I'd never stayed there overnight *alone*.

As for the house, surely it was unnecessary. Plus, Henny wouldn't know if I didn't keep that promise. But I'd know. So there it was.

I was such a sucker. Meaning well and caring had only ever gotten me pulled into situations I resented. *Every. Single. Time.*

Home first, then, because I'd have to grab a few more things for the night.

❧❧❧

I camped on the narrow, old-fashioned chintz daybed in the sunroom at the far end of the house. Most of the bedrooms were upstairs, and if the beds had sheets on them . . . well, the sheets had been on them a very long time, so I gave those a pass.

I swung by my house and grabbed my pillow and blanket and a couple of books. That house, after dark and empty except for poor little me, would be like sleeping overnight in a dusty antique shop.

The daybed looked more comfortable than it was. I woke every hour on the hour, cursing the lumpy filling and sprung springs. When I woke for the last time at six a.m., I was stiff and achy. And yet I lay there. The walls of the dayroom were mostly windows. No view at night, but lovely early in the day. The sun was slow to rise, as I was, and I watched the sun's rays peek through the trees until it rose high enough above the horizon to gild the branches of the evergreens, and my mood improved.

Aunt Henny was coming back home today, and I'd try to make it a little special. But first, coffee and a shower for me.

Would the hospital call? Maybe. More likely, they'd call Lisa first. But the word would reach me at some point this morning to tell me to come pick up Henny, and I'd be ready.

⋘⋙

The knock on the door took me by surprise. No one knocked on the door here except for hired caregivers or service people, and none were expected this morning.

Maybe somebody was selling something?

I swallowed the last bite of my toast as I walked up the hallway to the front door.

The visitor knocked again. I peeked out the front window, then stepped back. I'd glimpsed a man. Just a partial glimpse. He was wearing jeans and a flannel shirt.

And I also saw the big black pickup truck parked near the front steps.

Coincidence? I thought not. I shrugged. There was only one way to find out what he wanted.

I opened the door a few inches, keeping my hand on the doorknob. "Yes?"

He raised his eyebrows in mild surprise to see me. I was *more* than *mildly* surprised when I saw *him,* and saw who was standing beside him—*a small, dark-haired boy.*

Chapter Four

The man's expression was a mix of surprise and doubt.

"You're the woman I spoke to the other day." He gestured generally in the direction of the subdivision.

"Standing in the middle of the road? Yes, that was me. *Daydreaming*, I believe you called it."

He took his cap from his head. His hair was thick and dark and could've benefitted from the attention of a comb, but his manner was polite. He said, "Sorry for disturbing you. I was told an old woman . . ." He paused and cleared his throat. "That is, that an elderly lady lives here."

"She does. I'm a friend."

"A Mrs. Hennipen, I think?"

He was tall. I hadn't been able to see that in the truck. A good six or seven inches taller than me. But he seemed safe enough, plus he was here with a child. Even so, my usual reserve with strangers prevailed.

"Yes, that's her, but she isn't able to come to the door just now."

I could see him thinking about what to say next. The boy spoke up, saying, "I have to apologize to her."

His manner, his words—they disarmed me. Especially the way he pronounced *apologize* as if the *olo* was fluid and uncertain. It also embarrassed me because Henny hadn't imagined her trespasser after all. That much was obvious. The rest of us had been wrong.

I said, looking down at the boy, "She isn't here just now. She's in the hospital. She might be home later today. I'll be happy to give her a message."

The boy looked away. I glanced at the man, who in turn touched the boy's shoulder.

"Show her," he said.

The boy's cheeks flushed as he began digging in the pocket of his jacket. When his hand came out, he held several red bows. One dropped from his hand to the porch floor. Swiftly, he stooped and grabbed the bow back, now holding the bits of red cupped in his hands.

I felt guilty. First, for not believing Henny. Second, because somehow the bows had been an irresistible lure for this boy and now he was, rightly or wrongly, being put on the spot, and my heart hurt for him.

"Oh," I said.

"These are from the lady's tree?" the man asked.

"Yes." I hurried to add, "It's okay, though. No harm done." I was thinking of the hundreds of ribbons I'd tied to the tree. I said, "He's welcome to keep them."

The man shook his head and grimaced. "No, ma'am. He took what wasn't his. He needs to put them back where and as he found them."

I heard certainty in his voice and read steadiness in his dark gaze. But not with meanness. Not even being harsh. Just a basic explanation.

I looked from him back to the child. "What's your

name?"

The boy opened his mouth and spoke, but so softly it was as if he hadn't spoken at all.

The man said, "Johnny. That's his name." He offered his hand to me, saying, "I'm Nathan Shaw."

After a moment of hesitation, I accepted his hand. Our shake was light and brief.

I said, "I'm Amelia Hennipen."

⊂⊰⊱⊃

I didn't invite them in, but instead suggested we walk around to the backyard. In my opinion, the boy's apology was sufficient, but when Mr. Shaw decreed the boy's punishment, I'd watched Johnny's small chin jut and his jaw tighten as he raised his head and stood straight. I suspected that the act of restoration might mean more to him than I understood. A step toward forgiveness or something like that?

"That's the tree back there, just inside the wooded area. That's where the red bows came from," I said.

He stared. "Yeah. The one with the red . . ." His voice trailed off, then he asked, "Not flowers?" He looked at me. "Ribbons?"

"The bushes nearby are camellias, and they'll flower again soon, I hope." I didn't want to say more. I knew how stupid it all sounded. But he continued looking at me, and a hint of a frown began to form on his face. So with a soft sigh, I said, "The red . . . yes, those are all red bows."

"Mind if we . . ." He gestured toward the woods.

When I hesitated, he added, "It's good for him to put the bows back, if you don't mind."

"Oh. No, I don't mind. If that's what you want, then go ahead." It seemed silly to me. On the other hand, maybe there was something more serious at play that I wasn't aware of. "Sure."

"Come on, Johnny. Bring the ribbons." He touched the boy's shoulder, and the two of them crossed the yard.

I watched them half vanish into the edge of the woods. It unsettled me. As if strangers were trespassing on my territory or interrupting a . . . ritual? No, maybe more of a tradition. It was just ribbons, after all. No big deal, really.

They were gone for only a few minutes. They walked side by side, stopped short of the bridge, and Mr. Shaw knelt and seemed in close, earnest conversation with the boy. One nodded, and then the other. Mr. Shaw stood and the two walked the rest of the way back to where I waited, but as they passed the broken swing set and the rotting sandbox, I noted how the man's eyes touched on them.

My annoyance was now fueled by embarrassment. Not for me, but for Henny. For how she still viewed the place of her childhood, which now—through the eyes of this stranger—had lost even the ghost of its charm, of family memories. By the time they reached me, I was done with conversation. *Enough.*

"So, umm . . . Mrs. Hennipen . . ." The man scratched his stubbled cheek.

"Look, Mr. Shaw—"

"For the boy's sake, if you don't mind, should he call you Miss Amelia or is Mrs. Hennipen better?"

"Miss Amelia." This all felt very foolish and unnecessary.

"Johnny and I discussed this, and we agreed that there were two . . . uh, *errors* made. Taking the bows is one, yes, but to do that required coming onto other people's property without their permission, right?"

Johnny and I nodded, almost in unison.

"So he and I think returning the bows only solves the one error but not the other. We're thinking we should—"

"No, please." I waved my hands to shush them. "Nothing more is needed. I understand what you're saying, but it's all good."

He gestured at the boy, saying, "Go sit on the steps . . . back there on the porch. Don't move. Miss Amelia and I are going to talk."

Johnny did as instructed, but I bristled. I didn't like this man's tone, not one little bit. But when Shaw moved a few steps farther away and even lowered his voice, I actually moved with him to hear him better. With a look on his face that I couldn't quite read, he asked me, "Why?"

I'd lost the thread of this conversation. "Why what?"

"The bows. Not my business, of course. Just asking."

"*Why?*" I lifted my chin and discarded my confusion. Coolly, I said, "For Mrs. Hennipen's grandson."

"For . . . So she ties the ribbons on the tree?"

"No, *I* tie them."

"For her grandson?"

No more, I thought. I turned away abruptly, fully intending to leave him there, both him and the boy. They could be on their way now with my blessing.

"Wait, please, ma'am. I mean, Amelia, if that's okay?"

I paused.

"Apologies for asking questions. Touched a nerve, I guess. I just wanted to understand."

I turned partway around.

The man nodded. "Now I do, and I can explain to Johnny why he shouldn't mess with the tree and the bows. It *should* be enough to just tell him to stay off the property—to not go where he's not invited or welcome—but well, Johnny, he's young, plus he has some issues. A good kid, but he . . . he sometimes just does . . . stuff. He doesn't stop to think." He grimaced. "He'll understand it better now, when I tell him that the bows are for someone she misses, and that's why he shouldn't take them off the tree."

A little regretful at having been so short with him, I said, "Thanks. Truly, I don't care about the ribbons and bows. The biggest problem is that when Mrs. Hennipen sees him out here it confuses her. Mentally, she's pretty together, but she gets confused easily . . . a little lost in the timeline."

"Pardon?"

A tiny smile forced my lips into something a bit

wistful. "Sorry. In the timeline of her life. She always enjoyed seeing the camellia blossoms and bugs me when they don't bloom as expected. I started tying the ribbons there after . . . well, after the holidays last year, and she thought it was blooms . . . and so I just kept on. Doesn't make any sense, I guess." I shrugged. "Especially to your son."

He coughed. "Not my son. My nephew. His mom . . . passed six months ago, so yeah, I think he'll get it. I hope so. If he doesn't, just let me know and I'll talk it through with him again."

Stunned, for a moment I couldn't find my words. While I was struggling, he asked, "Any kids here now? The equipment doesn't look used."

I shook my head. "No, not in a long time."

"Maybe she'd like it cleaned up?"

"She doesn't see it the way you and I do. She sees this all as she remembers it . . . back when . . ."

"I could haul it out of here."

"I don't—" I said, but then I broke off. "We have a guy who cuts the grass but that's it. He keeps it short to discourage snakes and such and so that it doesn't look totally derelict." *Shut up,* I heard in my head. *Shut up. Why are you saying all this?* I tried to pull it back with, "I don't think Aunt Henny will allow more to be done."

"Look, I'm not trying to push into your family business or drum up work, but it might be a good job for Johnny—a what-d'ya-call-it? A teachable moment. A good deed apology kind of thing for the trespassing part of what he did."

"What is it you think Johnny can do?"

"He can pull weeds or whatever while I get rid of the old swing set and that sandbox. They're not useful. Hazards, even. I have a truck. I'll take 'em off to the dump, and then your lawn man can cut the grass better too."

"Maybe . . ." But I didn't finish the sentence out loud. In my head, I thought, *Maybe it'll help Henny with her timeline . . .* "I'd have to ask her permission. Don't get me wrong. Personally, I think it's a great idea. I appreciate the offer. But can I talk to her first? She's in the hospital. Can I let you know?"

"Sure."

"How do I reach you?"

He dug in his pocket and pulled out a card. And a red bow. He handed the card to me, saying, "Just call when you know. And call me Nathan."

He put the bow back into his pocket. I didn't ask why.

"Thanks," I said.

"Sorry for the inconvenience . . . all this."

And suddenly, it didn't really seem inconvenient at all.

"Until Mrs. Hennipen returns home . . . it's not a problem. Then again, as you say, this yard has some hazards, so maybe it's better if Johnny doesn't . . ."

"No problem. I get it." He called over to the boy. "Let's go, buddy."

The kid jumped up and ran over. Together, the two joined hands and walked away. I stood there watching the tall man with his mini-me, both wearing caps and jeans and denim jackets. And it wasn't for this man, or this specific child . . . but a sense of loss nearly overwhelmed me. For what I had and didn't have. For where I'd found myself at this point in my life.

I was both sad and glad to be standing here alone, with no one to see. I needed to hide my face and my feelings from those who depended on me to be strong. To keep my own grief at bay, the grief that should've eased into a distant memory long ago.

Some days I was no better than Henny.

Chapter Five

At lunchtime, since I hadn't heard from anyone—not Henny, not Mom, not Lisa—about if or when Henny was being released today, I drove over to the hospital to see what was going on.

When I'd visited her the day before, she'd been sitting up in her bed, perky and watching television. Today when I entered the room, she waved at me, saying, "Come along in, Amelia. Have you seen this show? Is everything okay at the house?"

I was stunned. I walked in slowly. "You look good, Aunt Henny." In fact, she appeared more alert and engaged than she had in a while. If not for the bruise, no one would guess she'd been hurt in the fall.

"I'm feeling real pert and ready to roll, Meelya. Just need my dancing shoes." She wiggled her feet beneath the thin white blanket and laughed.

Meelya. It was what she used to call me. It was a fond reminder from my childhood of how I myself had pronounced my name. She'd used *Meelya* like an endearment through the years. I hadn't heard her say it in a while.

The nurse stopped behind me. She said, "You're not being released quite yet, Mrs. Hennipen. Doc says you'll stay another night . . ." She paused and gave Henny a smile before adding, "But he's happy with how you're doing."

I gave the nurse a look.

She said, "You're her granddaughter, Amelia?"

It would have been so much easier to simply agree and then the nurse would probably just give me the lowdown on Henny's condition without explanations, but the temptation passed quickly. I did skirt the line a bit, however.

"By marriage. I help take care of her. Her daughter is her medical power of attorney, but she's down in Florida."

"What's your name?"

"Amelia Hennipen."

"I'll be right back."

Okay was still rolling off my tongue as the nurse left.

I went to stand beside the bed. "Henny, I have a question for you."

She was looking so good, I felt sufficiently encouraged to propose the swing set removal plan to her.

Henny'd caught my expression, and whatever she read there gave her pause. She asked, "House okay? You're sure?"

"Yes, ma'am. I stayed there last night, just as you asked me to."

"The gelatin here is good. They gave me orange."

"Well, I'm glad to hear that. Henny, I have an idea. While I'm watching over the house, how about I tidy up the backyard some? Clear out some of the old unused stuff so Stu can do a better job of cutting the grass?"

She was listening but frowning. She was about to say no. I could tell because she was beginning to move her head back and forth in that age-old signal of denial.

I added quickly, "It'll open up the view of the garden. You'll be able to see the camelias better. In fact, we'll get rocking chairs for the back porch and . . ." I stopped because she wasn't listening. Her focus had wandered.

But I was wrong. She was staring at the television but not watching the show. It was as if she was envisioning her backyard right up there on that TV screen.

She hummed something tuneless, then said, "Well, maybe so." Turning toward me, she nodded.

I said, "Great. I know someone who'll help. I'll have a nice surprise for you when you return home—"

She interrupted, saying, "Not too much, you know. Just tidy it up so the camellias look nice."

"No worries, Aunt Henny. If you don't like how it turns out, I'll do my best to fix it back for you." It wasn't a lie, I told myself. I'd get her a new swing set if necessary. At least I wouldn't have to look at that awful broken set any longer.

She patted my hand. "You're a good girl, Meelya. Nice person and my friend. You'll do your best for me. I know that for sure."

Henny had approved.

That had been too easy. I hadn't misled her, had I?

I was oddly excited yet also apprehensive.

The nurse returned. She said, "Your name is on the

contact list. Looks like her daughter authorized it."

Finally, I thought. I said, "I'm amazed at how good Henny seems today."

"The improvement you're seeing is because of the hydration—older adults are usually on the edge of dehydration—but mostly because she had a UTI. They can affect the elderly in all sorts of ways."

"Wow. Yes, I've heard that." I looked at her. "I knew they were testing her for a UTI, but I didn't even suspect. I put her mood, et cetera down to her condition."

"Well, she still has dementia, but she'll be in a little better shape, at least for a while."

I nodded.

"The doctor will probably release her tomorrow. He's watching the brain scan because of the head injury when she fell."

"But she's doing okay, right?"

"All signs are good, but at her age . . . well, she's frail. With the head injury, the doctor is just being careful."

"Thanks."

◌◌◌

I struggled with whether to proceed with the plan.

What if clearing out the old junk in the yard set her off, or set her back into anxiety and confusion?

But what if . . . what if those items were part of what was keeping her stuck in the past?

The same was true for me. Seeing those items took me back each time I passed them—even though I'd seen them so often it might be happening on a subconscious level.

Would I feel better if that blasted rusting childhood play equipment was *gone, gone, gone*?

Oh yes indeed, I would.

What about Henny? How would it affect her?

Would she even notice? It was a guess either way.

I'd left her after lunch. There'd still be daylight to work in if Nathan responded to my voicemail and came on over to the house.

For now, though, as I waited to hear from him, I sat at the kitchen table. All these *things*—stacks of dishes, the old cookbooks on the shelf, the piggy salt and pepper shakers, and the round decorative tin plates on the kitchen walls, not to mention the faded wallpaper and the old dinette set. I remembered the stains, even, and how some of them had happened. It all brought back memories for me. How much more for her?

So if it was on me alone to make decisions for her, what would I do? Suppose she was my grandmother and I had the legal responsibility to make such decisions for her, would I do this? Yes, absolutely, one hundred percent. I'd have that rusting junk in the backyard hauled away— especially while I had a willing body with a truck offering to take care of it.

I didn't have much time to ponder the idea. The days were shorter this time of year, Henny would surely come home tomorrow, and I had a strong feeling that her watching the swing set and sandbox getting ripped out of their moorings and dragged off might be more than she could handle.

Nathan had still not returned my call. I put his business card into my pocket.

I wasn't helpless. I was perfectly capable of taking down the old metal tubes and chains, and I was certainly able to pull up the rotten boards of the sandbox. It didn't have to be done well or even prettily. I only needed to disassemble it and drag the parts around to the side of the house—out of Henny's sight—until Nathan Shaw could haul it away.

Even without a UTI, Henny's brain tended to reset. If the yard was already clear when she came home, I was hoping it would be less of an adjustment for her.

⚜

After taking a long look at the swing set and assessing the best approach, I decided I could do this. There was a ladder and a few tools in the storage shed. The shed was padlocked, but I knew where the key was kept. All I needed was a screwdriver and maybe a hammer. Gloves might be handy too . . .

Given the time of year and the shorter days, I was running out of daylight.

When I dragged the stepladder out of the shed and tried to maneuver it into a level position below the horizontal bar of the swing set, I realized I wasn't quite as strong as I'd been in my twenties. But, hey, I reminded myself—I was still this side of forty. I was in good shape.

I climbed it gingerly, worried about that soft ground and was relieved when I was able to reach up and steady myself with a hand on the horizontal bar. Another two steps up brought me near the top of the ladder, but I was high enough then to actually put my arm over that top bar. The problem happened when I tried to lean far enough to the right to reach the bolts that secured the bar to the uprights at that end, and I was forced to acknowledge I was no longer as agile as when I was a kid.

The ladder shifted as its feet sank into the high grass and soft soil, and began to topple. At least I had enough sense left to grab that horizontal bar and cling to it instead of falling with the ladder. In fact, my arms were over the bar, which pressed against my armpits and my chest, and though the bar was cold, I was okay for the moment. I peeked down. Honestly, it wasn't that far down to the ground, but the problem was still the ladder, now on its side, because unless I could ease my body and my feet down onto its aluminum frame, there was no way I could land on it without risking injury.

I hung there, considering how best to move my arms and shift my hands to grab the bar so that I could try to control my descent, when a voice called out. A man.

Nathan Shaw.

"You couldn't wait?" he said. "Didn't you get my message?"

Without fanfare or invitation, he put one arm around my hips and simultaneously kicked the ladder out of the way. And just like that—like I weighed no more than a feather—he set me back on my feet.

I glared up at him. He saw my expression of not-quite-outrage, and certainly of shocked surprise. He reached up and gripped the horizontal bar and gave it a shake. "Didn't want to risk waiting on good manners. You're lucky the metal didn't bend or yank loose while you were swinging up there. Could've been hurt."

Indignant, I countered, "It's not that high."

Was he trying not to grin? Whatever was going on in his head, he sorted it out and responded, "It's all relative, right? Even height."

"I wouldn't have been hurt," I insisted, ignoring the truth. I had indeed been worried about suffering a twisted ankle, or worse. But that smirk on his face . . . it grated on me.

"Ah . . . maybe not." He shrugged, giving in to my insistence. "Meanwhile, before I get started—assuming the job's still on—let's eat some burgers with Johnny."

"Yes, the project's still on, if you're willing." I let my annoyance, my pride, go.

We sat on the deck, chilly but chummy. Nathan downed a burger super fast, then left Johnny and me there to eat at a more normal rate, while he went to bring the truck around back.

Johnny and I watched as, in short order, his uncle tossed a chain over the bar, secured it, hooked it up to the back end of the truck, and drove forward, yanking the creaking, squealing remains of the swing set right out of the ground.

After that, and mostly by sheer brute force, he broke up the larger pieces just enough to fit them into the truck bed. For the sandbox, he used a tire iron to leverage up the remains of the rotting logs that had framed it for several decades and easily tossed them in on top of the swing set bits and pieces.

It didn't take more than fifteen minutes . . . twenty, tops. Less time than it'd taken me to fetch the ladder and tools from the shed.

"Wow," I said. "Thanks."

He nodded toward the yard. "Needs some cleanup still. The swing set was cemented in, but the cement wasn't mixed right, and it's mostly crumbled. Made it easy to get the A-frames out, but those chunks will be lawnmower killers and need to be dug up. Probably should fill the holes in too." He pulled off his work gloves and tossed them into the truck through the open window. "I'll drop by tomorrow and clean that up. Won't take long in better light."

"Want some coffee or tea?" *Stupid,* I thought.

But maybe he didn't think the offer was stupid, because he said, "Yeah. Coffee would be great."

I returned with our mugs. The air was chilly enough that the steam rose and spread along with the aroma. Nathan was sitting on the porch. Johnny was out in the yard, kneeling in the remains of the sandbox. Slim pickings there, in my opinion, but he seemed to be entertained digging up whatever dirt he could find and occasionally making noises that imitated a truck's engine *revving.*

"Thank you again," I said. "I don't mean to keep repeating myself, but I truly appreciate what you've done for us. The broken swing set being gone changes the view so much. The yard looks better, and when the grass is cut properly—"

I broke off because Nathan was frowning at me.

"Is something wrong?" I asked.

"I don't get it," he said, and then he shook his head and looked aside. "It's not my business anyway." He sipped his coffee.

"What?"

He turned back to face me. "Mrs. Hennipen's grandson, you said. Named Simon, right? You said he was gone. Left some time ago? Years, I'd guess from the way you talk about it. I'm trying to say that I applaud you for helping his grandma. But you and Mrs. Hennipen . . . You're not even related. Why is she *your* problem?"

Chapter Six

Nathan apologized, saying, "Sorry, I shouldn't mess in your business. It's rude. I just—" He broke off and cleared his throat before continuing. "I give you credit for helping Mrs. Hennipen, but I don't have the feeling that this is a paid job for you. Am I wrong? No? So why are you on the hook for taking care of her?"

He was correct—my choices and my arrangement with Henny weren't his business, and I was offended. Or I should've been, but apparently I wasn't. Which annoyed me still more.

Was I so very desperate to talk to someone? Why him? Maybe because he, too, had been drafted into an obligation that wasn't his, and he'd done it because . . . because he cared enough to alter his life for someone else? "No, I'm not paid, and yes, I devote a lot of time and energy to watching over Aunt Henny, but . . ." I spread my hands wide, palms up. "But I do it because I can. Because she needs me." I shrugged and put my hands on my thighs.

"You asked, *why me*? She was always kind to me. Aunt Henny treated me like one of the grandkids: Simon, her daughter Lisa's two children, and me. She was always thoughtful and fun. When . . ." I cleared my throat. Having begun, I dug in my heels. I'd get this said.

"When I married Simon . . ." I stopped again for a breath. "He and I were childhood friends. Teenage friends

too. We didn't become sweethearts until college. We got married right after college. He traveled a lot, and we hadn't settled down yet. Back then, I was here at this house with Aunt Henny quite often."

He made a noise—a doubtful-sounding *humph*.

"No, it was good. Really. Henny and I became friends. Actual friends. We synced." I smiled, remembering. "Sort of like partners in crime." I reached for the mug I'd set down beside me and sipped my drink, thinking of the late-night conversations with Henny through the years and our impromptu road trips for shopping, museums, whatever and wherever we chose to do.

"Eventually, Simon and I bought a small house over on the far side of the woods. A cottage, Henny called it. It was private, yet convenient, and Henny and I stayed close, and . . ." I searched for the right words to say and found only the raw truth. "And then he left. He said goodbye. It wasn't ugly. It was . . . like . . . anticlimactic."

I couldn't help the smirk I felt growing on my face, and I didn't understand it either. "But hey, he told me I could keep the house we'd bought together. Nice of him, right?" I trailed off.

"Thing was . . . as I said, Henny and I were friends, and we shared companionship when he was gone so much during our marriage, and again we shared our disappointment in Simon leaving us—like a two-person support group for broken hearts." I smiled, but the sadness crept up and around me again, as if never too far away.

"At any rate, she was fine back then. It wasn't until recently—over the last couple of years—that her cognitive problems became noticeable. Over the past year, she's been getting worse. Worse, but not totally incapacitated," I insisted. "She still has good days, and she never objects to having help here. She seems to take our presence for granted, *our* being primarily me, Megan, and Bianca, but other caregivers come and go. I'm pretty sure Henny understands why they are necessary to her staying here at her home, but she doesn't want to discuss that part of it."

I was suddenly played out—out of words, at least. Later, I'd regret revealing all this personal stuff to a guy I hardly knew. Not at this moment, though, when I was empty of everything. I stared straight ahead for I don't know how long, and then I remembered *why* Nathan happened to be here. He'd done us a favor. A good deed we hadn't earned and he hadn't owed.

We owed *him*.

"Thanks again for your help."

He asked, "Are we done?"

Ouch. I felt that. So much for the cozy, personal conversation. "Yeah. Right. Thanks."

"Wait. What about the rest?"

I was already half out of my chair. "What do you mean?"

"Well, I know about obligations and such. After all, *no one* would've *planned* for someone like *me* to take on the care of a little kid."

"*Well*," I said, echoing his own *well*. "But you stepped in when your sister passed. You took on the responsibility for your nephew."

"Because there was no choice."

I asked, "There was no one else who could take him in?"

"Sure there was." He laughed, but roughly. "They were even less likely choices for the job than me."

He was making fun of himself, but I heard his worry.

"Johnny seems healthy and content."

"I'm not used to getting a kid off to school and getting home in time to feed him before bedtime, then rousting him out of bed again when it's still dark. Living by the clock." He ran his fingers through his hair—a gesture of frustration, perhaps. "He goes to a neighbor's house between the time he gets home from school and when I get home from work. Seems like I'm always rushing, trying to fit into this new life." He added in a low voice, "He's a good kid. He deserves better."

I gave him a long look. He was staring out at the yard, more specifically at Johnny, who appeared totally satisfied, sitting in the last light of day in a used-to-be sandbox, digging in that sad pile of leftover dirt.

The boy was quiet. I'd never had a son. Or any child in my care. But even I knew little boys weren't usually this quiet. Maybe it was due to the loss of his mother.

I almost asked Nathan about her but then remembered we were more strangers than friends and our conversation had already been extremely personal. He'd mentioned his job. I was curious about that too. But I wouldn't ask today.

Maybe we'd have another conversation on a different day. Or maybe not.

Observing Johnny's contentment, I smiled. "Too bad the swing set and sandbox weren't in good enough shape for him to enjoy them."

"He's stuck inside too much. Can't be helped. Needs friends his age, you know?"

Don't we all, I thought. My only answer was a nod.

Nathan asked, "So he just left?"

I had a moment of blankness.

"Simon," he prompted.

"Oh." I grimaced. "Yes."

He said, "I'm divorced too."

I didn't know what to say to that. I told myself not to respond. Not to feel the need to correct this unofficial record of an idle conversation of the most painful, personal details of my life. I didn't owe anyone an explanation or justification for my life choices. I put my hands to my face and pressed my fingers against my temples, evidence of my own frustration. With a groan, I let the words spill out.

"No, we didn't divorce. He just . . . Well, a couple of years after he walked out, he died. The police delivered the news. He was living somewhere in Texas."

Shaking my head, I said, "Because of Simon . . . Because he never changed his will or his insurance beneficiary, I haven't had to keep a job, and I've been free to help Henny."

Silence filled the space between us.

I continued, "The divorce never happened. I wasn't trying to be evasive. If I say he's deceased, people offer condolences and then there's explanations and so on, so I just say he's gone. It's really no one's business . . . as you said. But it's not a secret either. In the end, it's just ancient history."

CR80

The next morning, after a call from Mom and another from the hospitalist, I dialed Megan's number.

"Megan, they're releasing her today. I'll pick her up, so no need for you to be at the house until after lunch."

"Sure thing. Gonna run by the grocery store on my way. Anything you can think of that I should pick up for her?"

"Whatever you think best."

It made sense that Megan did most of the grocery shopping, since she cooked most of the meals, some to be eaten immediately and some prepared ahead in case our schedule deviated from the usual.

We disconnected, and I left for the hospital.

They released Henny just before lunchtime. As we exited the main lobby, with an attendant pushing the wheelchair, she was full of chitchat about her adventure, as she now seemed to perceive her two-night stay there. The attendant guiding the wheelchair apparently had dealt with Henny during her stay because as we were approaching the exit, the young woman asked Henny if she still had her red bow.

I was out of Henny's line of sight. I wondered if she'd

forgotten I was trailing along behind her, because in response to the attendant's question, she waved her fist over her head and proclaimed, "Right here." She pressed her closed fist to her chest, adding in a tender voice, "A gift from my own sweet boy. He sent it to me so I'd know he missed me and was thinking of me."

Henny must've already shared this interesting little story with others because the gal didn't even blink, but turned to me and said, "So sweet. I love how one tiny ribbon means so much. Even the small things count. That's what I told my mom the other day . . ."

I stopped listening. I opened the car door and waited as the attendant maneuvered Henny into the back seat. They'd already told me the back seat was safer for Henny because airbags could do a number on her if they deployed. So, okay. That meant she was seated in the back seat by herself. Fine. It was a relatively short trip with plenty of scenery to distract her along the way. The belt was fastened now. Hopefully, it would stay that way.

Henny waved goodbye to the attendant as I closed the door. I thanked her myself and climbed into the driver's seat.

A gift from Simon? Had she really said that? I breathed deeply, trying to get my ire under control.

For reasons I couldn't express, it aggravated me almost beyond bearing, apparently breathing life back into the old anger I'd thought was buried.

Acceptance of reality didn't equal forgiveness. And how could I forgive him for something he'd never sought forgiveness for? He'd left without apology. That seemed to have been sufficient for him because I never saw or heard from him again.

Henny behaved beautifully on the drive home. She enjoyed the scenery, the music on the car radio, and we made it back to Hennipen House without incident.

We were barely inside when Henny lost her temper. She'd walked straight to the kitchen and was now yelling. I nearly fell as I sprinted to reach her. I found her at the window. That poor window over the sink. How much distress had played out in this very spot over the years?

I grabbed her. "Henny, what's wrong? What are you upset about?"

"Boy," she cried. "The boy."

Through the window, I saw Nathan out in the yard, holding a shovel. He was standing still and staring at the house. He'd surely heard that hullabaloo and probably thought someone inside was being murdered.

Henny was still pointing. For sure, she'd seen Nathan out there, but I doubted she'd seen Johnny in the yard from up here, but she kept repeating *boy* . . .

Suddenly, she was at the back door, yanking at the knob.

"Wait, Henny. Calm down. Let me tell you about our new friends." I rested my hand gently on her shoulder and leaned close to her.

"Friends." She breathed the word, sounding almost hostile.

"That's right. New friends." I kept my voice calm and low. "I wasn't expecting them to be here when we arrived. I think they must be eager to welcome you back home. Let me introduce them to you."

Henny stared at me, hard, her fingers still wrapped around the doorknob.

I'd known Nathan planned to dig out the cement chunks and fill the holes with dirt, but foolishly, I had not considered that they might be here when Henny and I returned. Despite my effort to stay calm, I was worried my face betrayed the panic inside me and that Henny could read it.

I put my arm around her back, saying, "Good thing we still have our coats and shoes on. What do you say that we go out there, and I'll introduce you?"

Henny looked down at her hand on the doorknob and relaxed her grip.

"The man out there is named Nathan Shaw. And guess what, Henny? There's a little boy here with him, his nephew. Both of them helped me clean up the backyard. Remember, we talked about that?"

She nodded, but barely.

"The boy is very quiet, but I think he wants to apologize to you about the bushes."

"Why?" she asked.

My heart sank. A realist would say that hearts don't do any such thing, but I swear mine did. It sank right to my stomach. Henny had had a reset. How much did she remember?

Carefully, I said, "He's the boy you saw messing with your bushes."

With strong movements that spoke almost of violence, she shook her head. "No."

"What do you mean, *no*?"

"*No*, it wasn't him."

And what does that *mean?* I thought about what she'd said to the wheelchair attendant.

Regardless, the two guys—one small and timid and the other tall and imposing—were out there, waiting, and I decided to go with it. I told myself I knew the right words to speak to her.

"The least we can do is to say hello to them. It would be the courteous thing to do. An act of kindness."

And that got her. The words reached inside and found Henny's essential, gracious heart.

I flipped the deadlock bolt and the thumb lock in the knob. She stepped back and I opened the door that led onto the porch, but then I moved aside and let her go out ahead of me—Mary "Henny" Hennipen of Hennipen House, preparing to welcome guests.

Maybe

Chapter Seven

We stopped on the back porch and stood near the railing as Aunt Henny scanned the backyard, silently searching for something or someone. The old swing set or the sandbox? She didn't even blink at the empty areas in the yard where the swing set and sandbox had existed just the day before. Her gaze passed over Nathan and Johnny and continued moving without pause until she fixed on the black pickup truck parked in her backyard. But that was only for a moment, and she didn't remark on the oddity of the vehicle being there.

Even the red dots of color visible through the evergreens didn't catch her attention.

Instead, she turned to me. She looked up, her faded eyes liquid with unshed tears.

Softly, she asked, "Simon?"

I shook my head. "He isn't here."

"*But he is*," she insisted as she unclenched her fist. She showed me the ribbon. "He sent me this."

Ignoring our audience, I took her hand, holding it as I gently curved her fingers back over the bit of red fabric.

"Henny, you know Simon loved you. But he can't be here." I nodded my head toward our visitors. "That boy down there, do you see him? He likes red ribbons too."

She reclaimed her hand, thrusting her fist into her coat pocket. When her hand reemerged, it was empty.

"Who is he?" she asked, indicating Johnny.

Finally, the constriction in my chest eased. My relief probably showed.

We stood at the railing. I pointed to Nathan. "This is Nathan Shaw, a neighbor, and that's Johnny, his nephew. They helped me tidy the yard."

Henny's breath sounded a little ragged, but she pulled herself together, standing taller. Before she could say more, Nathan moved closer to the porch steps. He reached up and touched the bill of his cap, tipping it ever so slightly. He said, "Ma'am. Mrs. Hennipen, nice to meet you."

What a voice—so at odds with this man's rough appearance. A warm voice. The tone reassuring. Even mellow.

With a gentle tap on the boy's shoulder, Nathan urged Johnny to speak.

Henny gave Nathan a long look and seemed unperturbed, but when she stared at the boy—first at his dark hair, then taking in his denim jacket and jeans, and all the way down to his boots—I sensed her confusion.

Johnny stepped forward, his small hand digging in his pocket as he climbed, step by step, up to the porch. His eyes were big as if he was frightened, and when he tried to speak, words failed him. But he didn't cower. Instead, he stopped on that top step and offered his hand, lifting it toward Henny, much the same as he'd tried to do when I'd first met him on the front porch. Then he opened his hand to show Henny his ribbon.

I hadn't anticipated that. It jolted me. But I stayed silent and prayed a quick prayer that the Henny I knew and loved would come through for both her and this child.

She reached down to take the ribbon from his small, slightly grubby hand. The boy dropped his gaze again as if he'd admitted to a great crime and he expected dire punishment.

Henny spoke sharply. "What's wrong, boy? Cat got your tongue?"

Her words were stern, but for me, the sound of those words in the voice I'd known all my life broke this fragile moment into a thousand glittery pieces, bright like confetti. And I laughed. Loudly. And then I put my arm around her shoulders and hugged her.

"I haven't heard you say that in years." Still laughing, I switched my attention to Johnny. "She used to say that to all the kids, including me—once upon a time, long, long ago."

Johnny looked up at us, his mouth gaping, probably marveling at our madness. Also in relief, I imagined, since clearly, there was no anger or punishment imminent here. And I wondered what his life was like. Something in me— pity?—stirred uneasily.

Sotto voce, I leaned close to Henny's ear and prompted, "Johnny."

"Johnny," she repeated after me.

The boy perked up.

"Go ahead, buddy," Nathan urged.

Johnny lifted his head to face her and said, "Nice to

meet you."

Someone had drummed that polite greeting into him. I could hear the learned-by-rote sound of it. But a change came over Henny.

She smiled. "Nice to meet you too, Johnny."

My relief was so huge that I exhaled loudly. Everyone must've heard the sound. I didn't care. I said, "Can I offer everyone cookies and milk? It's nice out here, and I think we're all due for a treat."

"Okay, yes, ma'am." Johnny nodded.

Henny was watching him and echoed his sentiment. "Okay."

I'd planned to bring the snack outside—it was certainly warm enough to sit on the porch in the shelter of the house—but Henny gave a hearty wave at our visitors, indicating they should follow her. She headed for the kitchen door. Johnny was right behind her.

Nathan paused when he reached me. "You're good with this?"

I nodded. "Yes, I think so. I *hope* so. She might slip and forget Johnny is . . . *Johnny*."

He shrugged. "If she does, I'll explain it to him later."

"Okay." I met his eyes, saying, "Then let's just go with it. Might want to cross your fingers for luck, though."

They settled at the kitchen table. I put the cookies out and poured a glass of milk for Johnny. Nathan, Henny, and I opted for tea.

Conversation was sparse. I didn't know what I'd expected, but all four of us just sort of stared at one another. Nathan tried to speak a couple of times, clearing his throat and never quite getting anything said, but Henny was only interested in watching Johnny take bites of his cookie in between him staring around at the walls, at the rooster clock on the wall, the teacup wallpaper, and so on. Nathan and I tried to chat, but we'd already exchanged some very personal details about our lives, and now, in Henny's kitchen, we couldn't think of anything to say. Maybe it was due to the faces of our tablemates. Henny was smiling but also staring—perhaps simply feeling awkward now that she had guests. And Johnny . . . well, he didn't seem to have a gift for conversation.

We were saved by the creaking of the front door hinges. It was amazing how that slight sound could sweep right up the hallway and into the kitchen. We turned as one to look in the direction of the kitchen door.

In disproportionate relief, like that of being rescued, I called out, "Hey, Megan. We're back here. Do you need a hand?" I turned to our guests. "It's Megan. She spends the day here with . . . uh . . . doing household tasks and such."

"Babysitting me, you mean," Henny fussed.

I ignored her core meaning and countered with, "Are you saying she doesn't do the cooking, the dishes, and—"

Henny waved her finger at me. "Now don't you be catty with me, missy."

I grinned at Johnny, who smiled back.

Megan swooped in with her usual energy and did a quick stutter step when she saw our company. She set the two grocery bags on the counter, then turned back to us.

"What's this?"

"We have guests," Henny said.

"Well, that's nice and all, but I'm talking 'bout those cookies." She put her hands on her hips and frowned at all of us. "Cookies for lunch? Am I seeing this right?"

I said, "It's a party to welcome Henny back home." I gestured toward the guys. "This is Nathan Shaw and his nephew, Johnny."

"Pleased to meet you," Megan said. In a quick, almost comic switch of mood, she made a face, and with an exaggerated nod, she said, "I wouldn't mind a cookie myself." She took one from the plate and walked on through to the laundry room, where we usually hung our coats and kicked off our shoes.

Johnny seemed fascinated by Megan. His gaze followed her as she left the room and lit up again when she returned. Nathan didn't seem to notice his nephew's fascination.

Megan was back. She reached down into the heavier, bulging bag and came up with a turkey.

I said, "Megan," then stopped myself. After last year's misery with the whole holiday thing, I hadn't planned to do all the . . . stuff this year, but Megan probably didn't know that.

"Yes, ma'am." Megan appeared to be answering me, but I knew she intended her words for Henny. "It's almost Turkey Day. Am I right?"

Henny frowned and pressed her lips together.

Megan looked at our guests. "Do you already have your turkey?"

Johnny answered, "No."

She winked at him and added, "Martin's Grocery has them on sale for the best per-pound price in town, if you're in the market for one." She laughed. "Get it? In the market for a turkey?"

Johnny grinned, but the rest of us were slow to laugh.

Megan shook her head. "Tough crowd."

Johnny turned to his uncle. "Can we get a turkey?"

His voice, though timid, was loud in the silence.

"Yeah, probably not," his uncle said. "It's just us two guys. It'd be a waste. We'll keep it simple."

Johnny looked away, his smile gone.

Nathan shifted in his chair. "I've never cooked one, buddy, but if you want turkey, I'm good with that. We'll find a diner and—"

And then Henny spoke in a clear, certain voice. "You can join us."

There was a quality to her voice that caused me to question whether she was certain about what she was inviting them to.

I said, "Henny, are you sure that's what you want?"

Nathan said, "It's uh ... okay if—" He broke off and tapped Johnny's shoulder. "We'll get going."

"No, please wait," I said. "I'm sorry. We're out of the habit of having friends over, that's all. Please?"

Nathan sat again. Johnny's eyes were wide open and watching all of us.

Henny's eyes met Johnny's. Speaking directly to him, she said, "We'll have turkey and stuffing and cranberries. And spoon bread. Do you like spoon bread? Meelya makes the best I've ever eaten."

Johnny said, "I don't know."

With a glance at Henny, then back at Nathan and Johnny, I said, "Well, Johnny, what do you say we find out?" I gestured toward Nathan. "That's if it's okay with your uncle."

CR80

They left soon after. Megan had insisted that Henny must have a proper sandwich—not a sandwich cookie—and Nathan said, "We should go."

I said, "I'll walk out with you."

I waited on the porch while Nathan got Johnny into the truck and fastened his seat belt, then he walked back to me. I spoke softly, saying, "I'm sorry you were put on the spot like that."

"It just kind of got out of hand, I guess."

"She may forget she invited you. She has moments of clarity as well as moments of utter confusion. Mostly, she lives somewhere in between. But she's still the essential Henny, and that means she's unpredictable. She always has been."

I crossed my arms. "Frankly, Nathan, last year, holiday-wise, it was awful. It was just us. Henny cried the whole time. I had to box up the decorations before we ever finished hanging them. I don't know how it will be for her this year. Plus, there's always the possibility she'll forget she met you or she'll start calling Johnny *Simon*. Anything is possible."

Nathan scratched the stubble on his jaw. "Maybe we should decline."

"If you don't want to risk it, I won't blame you. I don't want Johnny's feelings to be hurt. He's too young to understand what's wrong with her." But inside, I felt a growing disappointment.

"That said," Nathan added, "I think he'll be let down if we don't come for turkey, but it's up to you. I can talk to him and see how he feels about it. He's a quiet kid but he's smart. Thoughtful too."

I shrugged. "Talk to him, then. See what he thinks. Ask him if he can be flexible if Henny is having a bad day and he won't be hurt if she forgets who he is, or worse, if she calls him *Simon*. Let me know what you think." I paused, then asked, "You have my number, right?"

"I do. From when you called about clearing the yard."

"Call me. Let me know if you have any doubts about this."

He stared at me. Suddenly, and embarrassingly, I felt my face grow warm and knew I was blushing.

We both started to speak at once. I said, "Please. I'm sorry about this. About dragging you into our problems— mine and Henny's, of course. You have your life and Johnny's to work out. It's not fair that I'm taking advantage of you, and I'm so sorry—"

He broke in. "I'm not sorry." He offered a one-shoulder shrug and a rueful grin. "Look, this isn't what I was expecting, true… not what I thought bringing Johnny to your front door would lead to, but sometimes it's healthy to have easy shakeups in life." His smile grew broader as he reached up to reset the cap on top of his dark, shaggy hair. "Besides, we guys get a good meal out of it, right? And from what you said before about last year's holiday… sounds like you and Mrs. Hennipen could stand a redo."

With a tiny hesitation, he added, "One thing maybe I should mention." He must've seen my change in expression, because he said, "It's a small thing, and you can mention it to Megan as you see fit?"

"What?" I shrugged. "Oh, about Johnny? He seemed rather fascinated by her. I didn't think you noticed."

"Didn't want to embarrass the kid. Yeah, I'm sure he was thinking of his mom. She had a ponytail like that, and did that same kind of bouncing walk around the room when she was feeling good about things." He shook his head. "It's not a problem as far as I'm concerned, but if your Megan is going to feel awkward, maybe it'd be good to check with her."

He waited, his eyes fixed on my face.

What a kind man, I thought. Aloud, I said, "She won't mind at all. She has two children and a warm heart. I'll give her a heads-up."

He smiled, and his eyes seemed to light up. "So we're still on?"

What could I say? I couldn't think. My eyes were stinging, and my throat seemed to close. I found myself speechless in that moment. Instead of words, I offered my hand.

He stared at it, then took my hand in his much larger, rougher grip.

I said, "Thank you."

He nodded. "My pleasure."

So many things could go wrong. The list was almost endless. Yet, I couldn't repress a smile as I said, "I do most sincerely hope that it will be. *A pleasure, that is*, and for all concerned."

Chapter Eight

Red is the color of Thanksgiving, especially if mixed with yellow to make orange—the colors of gourds and pumpkins and cornbread and fallen leaves. Ivory is also a color of Thanksgiving—the color of damask tablecloths and Mama Hennipen's fine bone china with its silver trim and dainty blue flowers.

Two Days Before Thanksgiving

Henny asked each day, several times a day, "When is Thanksgiving?" Each time, her voice ended on a high, anxious, squeaky note that grated on my nerves.

Depending on who was on duty, Bianca answered, Megan answered, or I answered. We each explained how many days were left before Thanksgiving. The answer changed daily, of course. It was a weird sort of holiday countdown. Bianca handled it as she did most things—with a simple and straightforward response. Megan was patient, sometimes couching her answer in a joke. Each time I responded, I tried to be patient, but honestly, the repetition worried me and put me on edge. We were now two days pre–Turkey Day. When I arrived just after lunch to check on things, Henny was napping soundly, clearly exhausted.

Megan took me aside, whispering, "She asked *the question* again this morning."

"Which question?" I scratched my head. "The one about Thanksgiving Day? Or is she going on about *important papers* again?"

"You don't think she's hidden something? A bill or such that's gonna be a big headache if we ever come across it?"

I shrugged. "Who knows?"

"Well, in this case, it was the Thanksgiving question. Apparently, for her, two days before the big day triggers specific actions. She insisted I open the doors to the dining room and that the two of us dust. Oh, and boy, did we dust too—furniture, fixtures, windows, and floors. Don't you love the smell of lemon furniture polish? Anyway, Henny wandered off halfway through, and I thought she'd lost track of what we were doing." She shrugged. "But *oh no*." Megan paused, as if for effect, and waited for me to prompt her to continue.

"*And?*"

"*And* I found her at the old linen press pulling out tablecloths. I haven't seen tablecloths like that . . . maybe never. Fine old linen and lovely damask. Lace-trimmed napkins. Most definitely *pressed*, let me tell you. The creases from the fabric being folded and in that press for so long are pressed into that fabric for eternity as far as I can tell." She added with a little less zest and absolute seriousness, "I won't be trying to iron them out, no matter what she says."

"Okay then," I said, relieved. "We're still on for a

big meal with guests, and that's what's important." I smiled and waved my hand to encompass our increasingly festive dining room. "This actually makes sense. The old Henny would set the table the day before the holiday—whichever holiday it happened to be—just as her mama and grandmama did, so today she's tending to the dusting and the tablecloth. Once she's restored from her nap, she'll be pulling out the china."

"The china?"

I shrugged. "That's my guess. She'll be in here emptying the china cabinet out onto the table. She'll turn the plates and cups face down to keep them free of dust or whatever until mealtime on the big day." I was lost for a moment in my own early memories of holiday meals here at this house. The Hennipens had always done holidays just so—and thoroughly.

When had that changed? It had been a gradual lessening of family tradition as family engagement declined with the passing of generations. I remembered the good times, though, and wasn't sure whether being a holder of those memories was a blessing or a curse. You couldn't miss what you'd never had.

I *wanted* to lose myself in those memories. Of the good times. Of family and bustle. Of hugs and laughter and spats and more hugs.

Megan pulled me back into the moment, asking, "She's really going to do this, isn't she? And us with her?"

"You must've had some idea this might happen. You bought that huge turkey."

She laughed. "Actually, I'd picked that up for *my*

family, but my fridge at home is pretty full, so I was going to leave it here to thaw in Henny's spare fridge. And then, when I realized you were having guests, I bought a second one on my way home." She shrugged. "Hey, the price was right."

"I envy you."

Megan looked surprised. "What do you mean?"

I shook my head. "You'll be with your family. The idea of the four of us—two of whom were strangers to us just days ago—sitting around that table staring at each other, with me on edge, Henny confused, a little boy whose feelings might be hurt, and Nathan . . ."

Megan smiled. "He seems like a nice man." She shrugged. "You know what? Suppose we join you? Me and the kids. Ron won't get in until late, so we're having our official Thanksgiving the next day. The kids'll be happy to eat two turkey meals."

I felt as if she'd had thrown me a lifeline. I grabbed for it eagerly. "That would be wonderful."

"Should we ask Henny?"

"No. We'll tell her. *I'll* tell her—*if* you're sure that you don't mind joining us?"

"I'll come over early with the kids and get the turkey in the oven. What time do you want to eat? What about the side dishes?"

"Maybe we could eat at two o'clock? That's probably good timing for Henny. As for side dishes, what about . . ."

We had a quick menu discussion.

I said, "We'll keep it relatively simple." I paused,

then added, "Thank you, Megan. And you and the children can leave as soon as the meal is done. I'll do the cleanup. I'm staying over anyway. Bianca has a houseful for Thanksgiving this year and wants to spend it with her loved ones visiting from out of town. I'll be here tomorrow night and Thursday night."

"Nice. But that leaves you dealing with everything on your own starting tomorrow night, and the next, until Bianca comes back for Friday night."

"No worries allowed. Henny and I will be fine. I'll bunk in her TV room just as Bianca does. I'm a light sleeper."

"Tomorrow I'll pull out fresh sheets and a blanket and get the couch set up for you before I leave."

"No, ma'am, I've got it handled, just as I said."

Megan gave me that look . . . the one that usually preceded her warnings about how we were handling this caregiving thing. I wasn't oblivious to the potential issues, no, but we were doing the best we could—and Bianca and Megan made this balancing act possible.

She nodded, then shook her head. "One day at a time. No point in borrowing trouble, I suppose."

"You're a philosopher, Megan."

"No, Amelia. I'm just practical. There's no sense in borrowing trouble because tomorrow is sure to bring plenty for everyone all on its own—and the trouble a person gets is rarely the trouble they feared was coming."

CRSO

One Day Before Thanksgiving
The day before Thanksgiving, Henny was still asking, *How many days before Thanksgiving?* I believed her question was driven by her fear of missing the *right* day. I drove over that morning, parked in the circular driveway, and carried my overnight bag in. I stowed it in the laundry room. When I reentered the kitchen, Bianca was there, drawing on her coat.

"You'll manage okay without me?"

I assured her, "Yes, we'll do fine."

"Call me if you need me."

"Thank you, Bianca."

"This Thanksgiving event is very important to her. I'm sure you already know, but I wanted to mention it." She added, "Happy Thanksgiving, Amelia."

"Happy Thanksgiving to you too. Go enjoy your family and know how much I and Henny appreciate all that you do to help, to make it possible for her to continue living here."

A broad smile lit her kind face. "We do the best we can. That's all we can expect." But she stopped again at the door and said, "Make her laugh. Help her ease her worries by laughter, and maybe she'll get the day she's hoping for."

Megan arrived soon after. Henny pointed at Megan and me, took us each by the hand, and tugged us down the hall to the dining room. A set of dining room doors opened onto the foyer and across from the parlor. Another set was at the back of the dining room. The second set stayed closed because the room on the other side of those doors was used as Henny's sitting room or TV room. But the first set of doors were kept open these days so that Henny could keep an eagle eye on the decorations and the general state of readiness.

Did she think it might vanish when she wasn't looking? Maybe. In her present world, sometimes stuff did seem to do exactly that.

Henny hustled us along until we three stood in the dining room, and then, with a certain breathlessness, she asked, "What have I forgotten?"

I looked down at her and squeezed her hand gently. "It looks wonderful." And it did. I said, "The tablecloth, the napkins, the runner, a pumpkin crocheted in orange and green yarn as the main table decoration . . . everything looks perfect. But where did you find the pumpkin?"

Megan said, "Henny was sitting with it on her lap this morning. I've no idea where she got it. She insisted it belonged on the table."

"Someone crocheted it for her many years ago. I don't remember who. Doesn't matter. It looks cute there." I smiled. "So the only thing missing is the flatware. We need forks and knives."

"And spoons," Henny said.

"Maybe. We'll certainly need serving spoons."

"Mama's silverware. We always used Mama's silver." She looked up at me expectantly.

I hadn't seen "Mama's silver" since . . . *In years.* "The regular flatware will be fine, Henny."

"*Mama's silver,*" she said, her voice betraying a slight tremble. "I don't remember where it is."

"I don't remember either, Henny, but I'll try to find it. That's the best I can do."

She nodded, saying, "You'll find it. It's where important things are kept. Some of them, anyway. I don't remember what all is there. But *important*. Like *Mama's silver*."

If the elder Mrs. Hennipen's silver was still in the house . . . If it had been in the main living areas, I would've seen it or Megan would've come across it. There was a possibility it could be in the attic, but I didn't think so. I remembered the wooden box it was stored in. I even recalled Henny directing my attention to it many years ago. Something in the back of my mind told me that had been during the time when Simon and I were still married.

The family was already falling apart by then. People had moved away. I couldn't remember seeing the Hennipen silverware in place on the dining room table since.

There was the possibility that Henny's daughter, Lisa, had taken it after she moved away, but I doubted it.

So if the wooden case of Hennipen silver was still here . . . and if *I* were *Mama's silver* . . . I stood still and asked myself, *Where would I be hiding?*

At first, I felt foolish playing this old game of finding something lost, but then I had an inkling . . .

Megan had found Henny going through the old linen press.

The linen press was in a small, dark room, kind of a tucked-away pantry for forgotten things. There used to be a massive old mahogany sideboard in there too.

So that's where I went.

I found the wooden silverware case in the deep lower drawer of the sideboard. The box was sitting atop a slightly larger serving tray, and I fumbled with it in the awkward space, trying to pull the heavy box out without snagging what was under it, but I managed. While I was focused on the task, Henny came up behind me. She was excited and tried to reach past me.

I said, "Wait a minute, please, Henny. I think this is what you're looking for."

Her eyes went blank and her brows narrowed in what seemed to be confusion.

"Just bear with me, dear Henny. I've got it now. Let's take the box to the kitchen. Follow me."

We opened it on the kitchen table. Yes, it was the silver. That was the good news. The unfortunate news was that its silvery shine was buried behind a truly horrendous level of tarnish—on the last day before Thanksgiving and with guests coming.

Tarnish was the reason stainless steel cutlery had become so popular.

Henny's face had that confused look again, but it didn't last, because when she spied the silverware, she gasped.

"I'm sorry, Henny. It's badly tarnished. Let's just use the stainless utensils tomorrow."

Henny's fingers were still touching her lips, but the expression on her face was now one of genuine delight. "You found Mama's silver, Meelya. Remember when we used to clean it?"

I couldn't echo her delight.

"No, I don't recall. Maybe it was you and your—" I broke off. No need to remind her of the loved ones she'd lost, however long ago. "It's too bad, really, but we don't have any silver polish."

Megan must've been coming up the hallway when I spoke, because she called out, saying, "Check under the sink. There's an old container of it under there. Might still be good."

Aunt Henny laughed and clapped her hands.

I picked up a spoon, looked at the handle and its beautiful flowered pattern, deeply engrained with decades of tarnish, and sighed in dismay.

೦೩೮೦

Megan set us up with clean but threadbare washcloths we saved for utility purposes and an old dishpan with water for dipping the rags in and for putting the cutlery in after we'd gone over it with the polish.

She said, "I'll wash the utensils properly after you're done."

Our eyes met and she grinned.

"You two gals have fun with that project," she said with a wink at me.

I put an apron on Henny to protect her clothing, and I rolled up both our sleeves. If she could stick with this chore, who was I to fuss or refuse to help?

How much did we need to clean? One set of utensils

for Henny, one for me, one for Nathan, and one for Johnny, then a set each for Megan and her two children . . . equaled seven place settings plus the serving pieces.

I said as much to Henny, who added, "Add some extra in case someone—like maybe one of the children—drops their fork on the floor?"

Inwardly I groaned, but outwardly I agreed. "Yes, ma'am."

Megan laughed, and the doorbell rang. "Are we expecting anyone?" she asked.

"Not that I know of."

I heard the hinges, then Megan spoke and a man responded. I couldn't make out their words, but I recognized the man's voice.

Was he backing out the day before the big meal? Better than the day of, I thought. I was surprised by how disappointed I was, and not just for me. For Henny too.

Footsteps came up the hallway. Both sets. I paused mid-cleaning; I watched the kitchen doorway. Megan came in first. Nathan was right behind her, holding a stack of white pie boxes.

"Good morning," he said in greeting. "Got a good deal on these. Hope you don't mind me contributing."

He set the boxes on the counter. Just simple white cardboard, stacked neatly—nothing remarkable.

When he asked Megan if it was okay for him to leave them there, she said yes. I thought, *Hey, they're just pies. A friendly gesture in return for the dinner invitation. Just dessert. Nothing more mysterious or meaningful than that, right?*

Chapter Nine

Aunt Henny had looked up immediately when Nathan entered the kitchen with the pies and set them on the counter. When he turned to greet us, she stood, excited, but wasn't quite sure what to do with the spoon, fork, and rag she was holding.

"Pies?" she exclaimed. "I love pies. We always have them for Thanksgiving and at Christmas too."

Nathan said, "Yes, ma'am. We did the same when I was a kid." He added, "There's pumpkin, apple, cherry, and chocolate. Wasn't sure which you'd prefer."

"All of them," Henny said, sounding for all the world like a six-year-old girl on the eve of her birthday, but then she looked Nathan directly in the eye and said sweetly but very courteously, "Thank you so much for bringing them. We *shall* enjoy them."

He pulled off his cap and nodded politely. "Least I could do, ma'am." He gave me a quick glance as if checking that all was well, and then he continued speaking to Henny. "Mrs. Hennipen, my nephew and I are looking forward to joining you for dinner tomorrow."

"Thanksgiving," she said. "My favorite holiday."

"Yes, ma'am." He saw the mess on the table. "Cleaning the silver?"

I waved at the tarnished cutlery and at the wet rag, dark with the cleaning, and grimaced.

"Need any help?" he asked.

"Seriously?" I was sure hope lit my face.

Henny laughed.

"Absolutely," Nathan answered. "I'm off work today, and I've got some time before I have to pick up Johnny." He held Henny's chair for her, saying, "Ma'am?"

My dear Aunt Henny took her seat again with the assistance of Mr. Shaw—simpering for all the world like a new duchess at a fancy dinner party.

I laughed despite myself.

"Have a seat, Nathan." I handed him a clean cloth. "Do you need instructions?"

He accepted the cloth and the chair. "I can handle it."

Henny grabbed a butter knife and started wiping it down, but she'd forgotten to add more paste on her cloth. I reached across and gently directed her hand with the cloth toward the jar.

She looked at Nathan, perhaps shyly. "Who are you?"

Nathan paused before responding, and when he did, he said evenly, "A neighbor, Mrs. Hennipen. Name's Nathan Shaw."

She giggled. "Neighbor. Yes, I remember. You're coming to dinner tomorrow for . . ." She frowned. "Tomorrow, right? Thanksgiving?"

He smiled at her, and it transformed his face. The

rougher edges melted away and simply became strong features, and his eyes lit up. Lit with kindness, I thought. He touched his cap and then caught himself, instead removing it from his head and setting it on his thigh. Self-consciously, he mussed his hair, maybe because his hair felt different, as it should, because I could see he'd gotten it trimmed. It looked good.

He responded to Henny's anxious question. "Yes, ma'am. Thanksgiving is tomorrow."

Henny gave a loud sigh. "I'm so glad. *Tomorrow*. Sometimes my memory isn't what it used to be. I suppose you know that. Everyone seems to . . ." Her words trailed off in a mutter. Then she added in a clear, sure voice, "I don't want to miss it."

"No, ma'am, we certainly don't want to miss it. Johnny, my nephew, is very excited. His mom put a lot of effort into holiday meals and decorations and all that until she got sick. This is his first Thanksgiving without his mom."

Henny sat quietly for a long moment and then laid her cleaning rag on the table and reached over to touch Nathan's hand. "Tomorrow," she whispered.

ল৪৪৩০

Thanks to Nathan's help, we were done polishing in no time. His hands were large and moved with efficiency and deftness.

"You're quick, Nathan. Are you a professional

silver polisher?" I teased.

"No, ma'am." He smiled. "That said, I'm good with my hands."

Megan happened to be passing through the kitchen with a load of laundry and spoke out. "Guess we know who'll be doing the carving . . ." Her chuckle trailed off as she vanished down the hallway to Henny's bedroom.

Nathan looked a bit chagrined. "Well, I've never carved a turkey."

I said, "It's okay if you don't want to. You're a guest, you—"

He interrupted, "Never having done it doesn't mean I can't." He grinned. "I'll find a video online and figure it out."

I nodded, smiling back at him.

Henny asked, "Where's Johnny?"

Before Nathan could respond, I jumped in, suggesting, "In school?"

He said, "No. When I was a kid we had school for a half day the day before Thanksgiving. Seems like now the kids get the whole day off before and after Thanksgiving."

"So where is he? If you don't mind us asking."

"Don't mind at all. He's at a birthday party for a kid in his class. I have to pick him up in a bit, so I guess this is the end of my silver polishing career."

Henny laughed.

I asked him, "Since we're being nosy . . . what do you do? If not professional silver cleaning or polishing, I mean?"

He made a small noise I couldn't decipher. He said,

"Machinist." He shrugged. "Sorry, that word covers a lot of territory, I know. I make things with metal to do special jobs. Some designing. Some fabrication. When I came to Crimson Grove to help my sis and her son, I got a job at Owens Machine and Tool. It's closer into town—nearer the city, that is. So it's a commute. That's why the neighbor watches Johnny after school."

I thought of him uprooting his life. Starting over in a new place, a new job, for his nephew. I wouldn't want to have to do that. Neither of us were kids. Change didn't get easier with age.

In a more thoughtful tone, I asked, "Do you like it here? And at the new job?"

"There's good and bad everywhere. But it's okay here. I find I'm liking it better every day."

I wanted to smile, but I felt awkward. Seemed to me there was a certain subtext to his words. Was there? Or was it my imagination?

He meant exactly what he said—that and no more. Plus, I'd become aware of Henny watching us. Her eyes were on me, then Nathan, then me again, as he and I talked. It was a bit unnerving. Seemed best to conclude our conversation with a simple, innocuously polite statement.

"It's always good to give a new place a chance, to get to know it."

Henny made a rude noise. She tossed her cleaning cloth aside and slapped the table. "Well, that's it for me." She grumbled good-naturedly, "Nasty job, ain't it? Time for a nap." She stood but didn't move right away. "Gotta let the feeling come back into my legs. No falling today.

Am I right?"

"You are right." I rose from my chair. "I'll help you get settled for your nap."

This time Henny made a louder, ruder noise. "No, you won't. I'm not a baby. You stay here and talk to this man." She muttered, "Something more interesting, if you can manage it." She gave him a look. "What's your name?"

"Nathan Shaw, ma'am."

"Thank you for your assistance, sir." And she hobbled away, seeming slightly disjointed in her walk, as if her metaphorical springs were winding down. Megan was suddenly there, putting her arm through Henny's as they moved away, saying something about washing her hands.

"Naptime," I said softly to Nathan. I eased back into my chair.

"She's something, isn't she?" His eyes shifted from the doorway back to me.

"She is and always has been."

"It's hard, I know."

"What—" I frowned. "Oh, you mean because she's . . ."

"I watched my sister get sicker and weaker."

"Cancer?"

"Actually, no. It was a heart problem. The decline was like a new grief every day."

I wanted to say something wise, or maybe clever, but I couldn't come up with the words, so we sat together in silence.

Finally, I said, "Shall I walk you out?"

He nodded.

We rose together and stepped quietly, wordlessly, past the door to Henny's room. When we reached the open doors of the dining room, we paused. I thought he must surely have seen the room when he arrived, but maybe Megan and the pie boxes had gotten in the way.

He gave a low whistle. "Fancy."

"Nice, right?"

"Johnny's eyes are gonna be bulging. Are you sure you want a kid in there? I mean, he's neater than some, but—"

"Of course he's wanted. As a matter of fact, Megan's two children will join us also, so he won't be the only young one here."

We moved on to the front door, and I walked outside with him but stayed on the porch as he went down the steps to his truck. He paused as he was about to climb into the cab and lifted his hand in a wave. I returned the gesture and watched as he drove away.

I stood there staring at the long drive leading away from Hennipen House and at the truck as it grew smaller. Beyond the boundaries—and the forest and other greenery that gave the property its privacy—lay the wide world. As Nathan's truck vanished around the curve of the drive just before it reached Maple Street, it seemed to me that it might as well be another, separate world . . . and that somehow . . .

Somehow I'd gotten a little lost with one foot in each world—the world here and the world beyond these boundaries.

It occurred to me that by walking the forest path from home to here, I could effectively separate myself from that world . . . except for occasional excursions into it for groceries and doctor visits and such.

It gave me a shiver.

I shook it off. I ran my fingers through my hair and straightened my sweater. There were bits of cleaning paste on my sleeve.

Humph.

We'd made a mess on the table. Megan would think we'd left it for her to tend to.

Feeling steady again, understanding where I was and having tasks to do, I went inside and got busy doing them.

಼ಢ

Later that evening, long after Megan had left for the day, and Bianca was taking this night and the next off to enjoy her visiting family, after Henny was in her nightgown and tucked in and sleeping the sleep of an exhausted eighty-six-year-old, I decided to return the silverware box to the sideboard. I'd have to pull it out again to put the silverware away after our Thanksgiving Day meal cleanup, true, but we were going to need all the kitchen counter space tomorrow.

So I carried the box back to the small, dusty room and set it carefully on top of the sideboard among other abandoned treasures, while I fidgeted with the slightly off-kilter drawer to open it.

There was that tray I'd seen earlier. A nice large serving tray. We might find a use for that tomorrow—perhaps for serving pie? *Yum.* I removed it from the drawer, and when I did, I saw an envelope—a large manila envelope with one of those strings that wound around buttons to secure the flap.

Curious, I picked it up. There were names written on the front of the envelope in pencil, in a spidery cursive hand.

Mary "Henny" Hennipen. Simon Hennipen. Amelia Hennipen.

A chill hit me. I placed the envelope back in the drawer so fast, anyone seeing me might've thought the yellow paper came with razor-sharp claws and jagged teeth.

Yeah, I remembered this. Hadn't seen it in almost twenty years.

I grabbed the silverware box and dropped it in the drawer on top of that envelope, then slammed the drawer shut, or would've if the fit had allowed. Whatever was out of alignment was probably worse now after my rough handling. The drawer was a little crooked on the runners now and not flush with the chest. I'd come back later to fix it. Or maybe tomorrow.

Leaving the serving tray in the kitchen, somehow I ended up in the dining room sitting at the end of the decorated table, staring at the fixtures in the semidarkness. The light from the small lamp in the foyer streamed in, glinting here and there on the various shiny surfaces, giving the room an otherworldly feel.

I made myself remember. Forced myself to see the memory.

On the occasion of our fifth anniversary, Henny had her attorney draw up a document giving Simon Hennipen House on her death. It was written up as some kind of trust. Less than two years later, Simon walked out of our lives.

What if he'd stayed? What if we'd made our life here with Henny as she'd wanted? What if he hadn't died?

She'd raised him as if he were her own son. She'd always wanted Simon to have the house. He'd thwarted that plan by dying. And because he'd died before me, the house and property would go to Lisa. And that was probably as it should be. I didn't blame anyone for that. What would I have done with this outdated, impossible-to-maintain behemoth of a house?

I remembered the elder Mr. Forester. His name was . . . Benjamin. Yes, Ben Forester. He was a well-known local attorney who'd worked with the Hennipen family in their legal matters for many years. He'd drawn up the necessary documents. Henny had insisted that Simon and I accompany her to this particular visit with Mr. Forester. I'd tried to listen carefully as he explained the purpose of the trust, the details, but what did I recall most clearly? It was his hands, his fingers, swollen and twisted with arthritis, and thinking how it must hurt. But his mind was still sharp. I remembered that too.

He was long gone now. His son, Benjamin Jr., had taken over his father's practice. I presumed he was still practicing law. But as for the trust—in the end, with Simon gone long before his grandmother, Mr. Forester's efforts served no one. Well, except for Mr. Forester's earning his fee for the paperwork.

Why had Henny kept her copy of the document all these years?

Because that's what she did. She kept everything. Or tried to. But she was really doing no more than wrestling with time.

ℭℬℰ�

I checked on Henny before climbing into my own bed on the couch. The doors were double locked, and unless she had a bad dream or some sort of scare in the night, she wasn't likely to get into trouble. I was generally a light sleeper, but it had been a long time since I'd stayed overnight with Henny.

As far as I knew, all was peaceful that night until four a.m. when I woke.

There'd been no noise that I was aware of. I simply realized I was awake, and I was startled to see Henny sitting on the edge of the recliner seat with her hands clasped in her lap and her eyes boring holes into me.

Watching me sleep, maybe?

I asked, "Why are you up and awake at this hour?"

"It *is* you. I wondered. Thought maybe I was still asleep and dreaming."

"It's me."

"Where's Bianca?" she asked.

"With her family, getting ready for Thanksgiving."

"Oh."

"Thanksgiving is today, Henny. But not yet. It's still dark. Do you think you can go back to bed until daylight?"

"Bianca gets me a drink and turns music on for me."

"Does she?" I pushed my blanket out of the way and sat up.

"What would you like to drink? Rather, what does Bianca give you to drink?"

Henny grinned. "Juice." Without missing a beat, she added, "And a cookie."

I gave her a doubtful look. "And then you'll go back to bed and stay there?"

"Of course." She said smartly, "We have a big day today."

Chapter Ten

*T**hanksgiving Day*
We started Thanksgiving Day especially early that morning. Not only because Henny was an early riser, but because, much like Henny, I felt the need to verify with my own eyes that this was *the day* and that the dining room, shining with all the special touches of the holidays, was as ready as it could be and hadn't come undone or vanished altogether, and that no one's present state (Henny's) had reset under the pressure of anxiety or excitement.

Check and check and check. Everything was as it should be.

I persuaded Henny to focus and eat her breakfast because she was going to need her energy and had to fuel her body and so on. In short, I told Henny that if she wanted to enjoy Thanksgiving, it was her responsibility to be well rested and well fueled. Henny complied.

On the other hand, Henny wasn't talking much, but she was muttering a lot under her breath. I suspected she was desperately trying to hold on to the day, worried that she'd somehow blink and discover she'd missed the event.

Between encouraging Henny to eat breakfast, helping her dress nicely for the day, and tidying her hair, I had my hands full. When Megan arrived with her children, she took one look at me and sent me to grab a shower and

pull myself together.

"Morgan and Bea will sit with Henny and either entertain her or just keep an eye on her, depending on what she needs. They'll be a nice distraction for Henny. But you look done in."

I did feel a bit crazed. "It was an early morning for us, and a busy one."

"Go now while you can. You have guests coming in a few hours, and we have cooking to do."

☙❧

The shower and the time alone restored me. I didn't overdress, but did choose slacks over my usual jeans, and a white cotton shirt with a dark green sweater with appliqued autumn leaves. When I walked into the kitchen, I felt appropriately seasonal, and ready. Ready to cook. Ready to entertain. Ready to enjoy the day.

The aroma of roasting turkey filled the house. Between us, Megan and I prepared the stuffing, the gravy, the cranberries, the broccoli-cauliflower mold. I made Spoon Bread. It was my favorite and my specialty.

For most of that time, Henny sat in the kitchen watching us. She was still relatively silent. Even the kids, Morgan and Bea, let her be. I'd never seen her so intensely focused.

At one point, I glanced over at the kitchen table and she was gone.

"Where'd she go?"

Megan called out, "Morgan, where's Mrs. Hennipen?"

Surely no more than two seconds had passed before he was standing in the doorway giving his report. "She's in the dining room."

A shot of alarm went through me. "Doing what?"

"She's just sitting at the table. She's not doing anything."

Afraid that she might start *undoing* our work, I turned to go check on her myself, but Megan stopped me. She said, "I'll go. I'll see if she'll take a short nap. She's too wound up."

Nodding, I agreed, though I had mixed feelings about it. If she *did* take a nap, and if she slept *too* deeply, the risk was greater that she'd reset. On some level Henny knew that, too. Getting her through this had become so desperately important to me ... On the other hand, a wound-up, overly stressed Henny wasn't a good choice either.

When Megan returned, she said, "She's resting now. Bea is holding her hand. Henny made her promise to keep holding it until she woke." Megan sniffed. She touched the hem of her apron to her eye.

My own eyes stung.

I had to cough to clear my throat before I could ask, "Is Bea okay with that?"

"She is. She's fine. Henny probably won't nap for

more than a few minutes anyway. I guess . . ." She cleared her throat. "Bea will be her anchor while she rests."

"But to ask a child . . ."

She shook her head. "I didn't. Bea and Henny worked it out between them."

I nodded. "Then we'd better get back to work. I'll line up the serving dishes and utensils on the kitchen table. Sound okay? What else needs doing?"

03&80

Henny was awake. Her nap had been short but effective, and we were all pleased when we discovered that it was still Thanksgiving Day in Henny's world. Impulsively, I kissed her cheek and then kissed the top of Bea's silky blonde head. The child giggled and Henny smiled.

The house was pleasantly warm and filled with the cooking aromas that proclaimed Thanksgiving. I turned on the dining room chandelier, and then one by one, almost ceremoniously, I turned the dinner plates and cut crystal drinking glasses right side up.

Now, we were ready.

Our other guests arrived a few minutes early. Nathan and his mini-me, Johnny, rang the doorbell, and when I opened the door, they were standing there with their hats in hand, their hair neatly combed, jeans clean, and boots shined, and I felt . . . oddly proud . . . as if, in some way, they belonged to me. That they'd done this *for us*.

Because they had. They might get something out of this day—at least a good meal—but I believed that we would be the true beneficiaries.

CRⱭ80

The dinner went beautifully. The memory of it was generally a blur.

We started shortly before two o'clock and were done eating in no time—as the best Thanksgiving meals happen—but we lingered after, the kids in the TV room and the grown-ups over coffee. I'll never forget Johnny's big eyes when he first saw the dining room in all its glory, nor Nathan's big laugh when all of us offered advice about turkey-carving techniques.

I know there were missteps, and yes, more than one child, including the child at heart—Henny—dropped a utensil on the carpet and needed a replacement. She was embarrassed. Her cheeks turned quite rosy. But then Morgan, who was the eldest of the three young ones—all of twelve years old—lost his fork too. Then Bea. And then, with the biggest grin I'd yet seen on Johnny's face, he dropped his spoon. It bounced on the carpet.

We all came together again when Nathan carried in the tray of pies.

I cannot begin to describe the laughter. The joy. It touched each of us, and for Henny and me, it dispelled the damage that last year's sad season had wrought. She and I caught each other's gaze. We knew we'd hit the jackpot when it came to the best Thanksgiving ever.

After dessert, everyone hung around, but even the youngest among us could see Henny's exhaustion. She'd grown pale. She tried to keep a smile on her face, but it faltered as she struggled to stay alert.

Nathan suggested it was time for him and Johnny to go, to sleep off the turkey, as he phrased it. Johnny had enjoyed his time with Morgan and Bea, and he was reluctant to leave, but then Megan said she and the kids would be leaving soon too.

Henny and I saw our guests out one by one. Nathan and Johnny went first. Then, instead of leaving, Megan suggested she should stay and help me get a start, at least, with the cleanup. I insisted that she'd done enough.

After Megan and the kids left, Henny and I went to the kitchen. I'd thought she could keep me company while I rinsed the dirty dishes. I was mistaken. Her head was bobbing, her chin dropping down to her chest, before I'd even gotten the dishwater hot and sudsy.

"Come, dear Henny." I took her hands. She looked up at me with an expression of surprise.

"Meelya?"

"Yes, ma'am, it's me. Time for a little rest. We've had a busy day."

"Not asleep . . ." That was as much as she could manage to express.

"No, Henny dear. Just take a catnap."

Her breathing got heavy, but she nodded. Even so, as I settled her in her recliner, she tried to get back up, then, finally, she gave in.

When I draped the sofa throw over her, she watched me silently. With sorrow, I recognized the confusion growing in her eyes. I took her hand between both of mine.

"Henny? Did you have fun today?" I wanted that response—that recognition of what we'd shared. But I didn't get it. Finally, I said, "It's all good, Henny. Rest now."

But as I tried to pull my hands away, she gripped them harder, refusing to release them until I'd leaned closer to her. My face and hers were almost nose to nose as I watched her lips moving without effect. Then she tried again, this time wetting her lips first. She patted my hand, whispering, "Christmas. Next."

I made it out of her TV room before I broke, and slid down the wall in the foyer of the Hennipen mansion, alone and strangely serene, until I hit the floor. Then I let the tears fall, rolling down my cheeks to drop onto my blouse.

When the tempest was done, I dried my lashes on my sleeve, then found my way back onto my feet. There were dishes to be tended to, and there was solace to be found in simple tasks.

There was also the truth that we'd had a wonderful Thanksgiving, yes. But the rest of the truth was that Christmas was only a month away.

Only.

I smiled. No laughing out loud for now because it might wake Aunt Henny, and I had chores to do.

Chapter Eleven

*B**etween Thanksgiving and Christmas*
Sometimes my mother called often, but we also went long spells without talking. Like me, she wasn't the sort of person who indulged in phone chitchat. Mostly, she'd call with messages relayed from Lisa, or, as I sometimes joked, she called to make sure I was still breathing and functioning. When I said that, she'd answer back—not joking—that I never called except on her birthday or on major holidays. It was sad but true. The saddest thing of all was that we didn't tend to enjoy even those small interactions with each other.

My emotional bandwidth was used to meet Henny's needs. Mom's was focused on Lisa's. They'd been friends all their lives. Much like sisters. And for me, Henny was like the grandmother I'd never known. For those few years when Simon had been with us, she'd been more like a mother to me than a grandmother-in-law.

I loved my mother, I did, but our relationship had never been the same since Dad died and she'd moved south. Her loyalties were focused down in Florida. Mine were here.

I called her the day after Thanksgiving.

"Happy belated Thanksgiving, Mom. Yesterday

was crazy, but in a good way, so I'm sorry I didn't get to call you on the day of. I hope your Thanksgiving was good?"

"Oh yes. Actually, Lisa finished her chemo treatment at the end of October and is doing much better, so it's all good news for now. How did your dinner go?"

"It went brilliantly. Some neighbors came, and Megan brought her children. We had quite a lovely time."

"How'd Henny do?"

"She had a blast."

"Really?"

"Truly, yes. We all did."

"That *is* good news. All the better because if Lisa's doctor approves, she and I are coming up for a visit— maybe in a couple of weeks. I haven't seen you in, what? Two years? And Lisa wants to see her mother. It will be all the better if Henny is lucid enough to actually interact with her."

"Mom, please." I drew in a deep breath. "She interacts even when she's not doing so well. She's still . . . her. I mean, she's still herself. Sometimes she's confused, yes, but—"

"Amelia, you don't need to worry. I've been around people with Henny's condition—same for Lisa. We know how this goes, and everything Henny's doctors have told Lisa bears it out. That said, it's good to set expectations, especially when it's a close relationship like mother and daughter. It's been very hard on Lisa not to be able to see for herself how her mother is doing and to not take part in caring for her."

That resistance I felt—as if someone was about to lay siege to my territory—was unbecoming to me. I drew in a deep breath and released it slowly before I responded.

"Mom, Henny is doing well. Lisa has done her best from Florida, especially considering her own health struggles. She's lucky to have you to help her. Henny is—I hope—lucky to have me. I'm good with it. Just as I'm sure you are with helping Lisa. Please tell her not to worry."

Our talk ended soon after. It left me with an unsettled feeling . . . a sense of foreboding. What was it that Mom had *not* said?

CR80

Nathan and Johnny helped me find a tree. We'd gone out to a tree lot run by a local charity. The lot was manned by volunteers and there was a booth that sold hot cocoa and coffee.

We stopped just inside the lot and I gave instructions: "Not too short because the ceilings are high. Not too tall because it's too hard to reach when decorating or taking the decorations down."

Johnny said, "Don't worry, Miss Amelia. I'll find the best Christmas tree ever. I'm good at picking trees. Aren't I, Uncle Nathan?"

Uncle Nathan confirmed he was skilled at picking trees.

Smiling, I answered, "Thank you."

Johnny took off into the lot so quickly that I called after him, "Don't get lost." I turned to Nathan. "Is he okay in there on his own?"

"He's fine. And I have a question for you. Before we take a tree to her, are you sure Henny wants this?"

"She's asking for a tree to decorate."

He maneuvered me over to the hot coffee and hot cocoa stand. Receiving the hot drinks from the young man behind the counter, Nathan offered me a warm cup of cocoa and kept one for himself. He sipped his, giving me an assessing look over the rim of his cup.

"Okay," I said. "I know she has memory issues. Judgment too. That's why she's not living alone. But even if she's not sure how long it's been since Thanksgiving, she remembers we had fun. She knows she wants to do it again. I seriously believe that this is what she wants. And . . ."

"And what?"

I tried to shake it off and move to a safe subject. "Last year was sad. This year, I don't see any signs of depression. She wants a tree to decorate. I wouldn't mind one myself. Where's the harm?"

Johnny was still wandering among the trees on the lot. I caught occasional glimpses of his legs and his boots between the trees and the people.

"Johnny wants a tree too," I added. "I don't think he'll mind helping decorate two of them, do you?"

"No. He won't mind." Nathan gave me another measuring look. "But you've been distracted all week. Something's on your mind. I don't want to intrude or push in where I'm not wanted, but if you want to talk about something, anything, I'll listen."

And he would, too. I didn't doubt it. We'd seen him several times since Thanksgiving, and each time it felt more and more as if I'd known him for years. I suspected he felt the same.

"Thanks. I appreciate that. There is something on my mind, but I don't want to discuss it just yet."

"Okay. Offer's open anytime."

Johnny was back. "I found the tree," he said. "It really is the best ever."

Nathan and I dropped our empty cups into the nearest trash bin and followed Johnny.

⋐⋑

That evening, when I was home—alone in my own small house on the far side of the woods—I could admit the truth. Since Mom's call I *wasn't* sure about having a tree, or about anything. I'd even dragged my feet about hauling out the Christmas decorations. What could've and should've been a fun time—even the fun of preparing for Lisa and Mom's holiday visit—had lost its joy for me. I didn't know how much Henny sensed, but I was pretty sure she'd picked up on my troubled heart.

My gloom wasn't fair to any of us. And besides, it was entirely possible I was wrong about what Mom *hadn't* said.

I'd always waited to hear whatever Lisa chose to tell

me—which information was usually delivered from her to me via my mom. It was a sort of protective culture of "let's not disturb Lisa because she's sick" that had encouraged the lack of direct communication.

And that was now about to end. We were just short of three weeks until Christmas. Time was running out, or so it seemed to me.

I dialed Lisa. She didn't answer, and so I left a voicemail. "Call me, please. I need to speak with you—*you directly*—about Henny."

She returned my call the next day, late morning. I walked over to Hennipen House, snug in my coat and scarf, and stopped at the camellia garden to tie a fresh bow on the sapling. I'd missed a few in the busy days before and after Thanksgiving, so I was adding a fresh one today and it was then that the phone rang.

"Amelia? Nice to speak to you. Sorry for all the times we didn't connect."

"No problem. I understood."

"What can I do for you?"

Well, Lisa was abrupt, yes, but she'd always been that way with me back in the day when we'd actually talked to each other.

I said, "Mom and I spoke just after Thanksgiving. She told me you were doing better and that you and she would be coming to visit. She said some things about Henny's situation and about my life too. It was what she didn't say that has been bugging me. I don't want to put Mom in the middle, but I need to know what, if anything, is going on that I should know about."

Lisa hesitated a few seconds, then said, "Yes, I supposed that's what you were calling about. I wish your mom hadn't . . . Well, she didn't actually tell you, but I can imagine the way she tap-danced around it roused your concern. Now that we're discussing it, I'll explain. Please don't say anything to Henny yet. I'd like to have that discussion with her myself."

I sat on the bench. "Tell me."

"I'll be moving Mother down to Florida in the new year so she'll be near me."

My breathing got loud, I think I even sputtered as I tried to figure out what to say. I knew Lisa could hear all that noise through the phone because she waited.

Finally, I was able to say, "I thought the goal was to support her in whatever way she chose to live, for as long as we could."

"Isn't that what we've done?"

"It's what *I've* done. It's what *we've* done with help from Megan and Bianca. You weren't part of that *we*. I didn't blame you because you had your hands full with your treatments, but how does it hurt you to let Henny continue on as she has for a while longer? Indefinitely. So long as we can keep this going?"

"It's not safe for Henny, and it's not fair to you."

"I haven't complained, have I?" I slapped the metal slats of the bench seat. "Henny and I are friends. I promised her . . ."

"It's not like she'll remember. We'll move her into a lovely, much safer, more appropriate living situation."

"But she won't be home." I tried to control my

anger. "That was the promise that we made to her."

"She'll be near me. The responsibility should be on me and no one else. It's expensive and difficult to get reliable help. Tell me—what's your plan if one day Megan or Bianca can no longer be part of the arrangements for Mother's care?"

I said, "As to the expense, it's Henny's money. As for the help, I'll find someone else."

"You'll try. I don't doubt that. But how long would it take?" She sighed. "Besides, it's about more than the expense and even the availability of caregivers. Good facilities are expensive too, and many are even more expensive than private care. But they have memory-care units—facilities where safety is a key part of what is offered.

"Mother is beyond the level of safety that can be provided at home. She is certainly a fall risk, as well as at risk of wandering off. And Amelia, you must think of yourself too. You have devoted yourself to this effort longer than anyone could have expected you to do. You did it out of love, I don't doubt that. But I only allowed it to go on this long because I was fighting for my life."

I ran out of words. Frustration and reality were beating me.

Lisa said, "It's time, Amelia. It's time to consider Mother's safety and your well-being." She paused. "I can do it now. I might not have the ability to manage this transition months from now, much less in another year. Life doesn't wait on us to get around to stuff when it suits *our* convenience."

I could almost see her holding her head high with that cool expression I remembered from my childhood, as if she had the upper hand and knew it. And she did, didn't she?

"I'll have arrangements made before the new year. When your mom and I come to visit before Christmas, I'll tell Mother myself. I'd appreciate it if you said nothing to her or the others before I have a chance to tell her the news."

I disconnected.

The cold of the metal bench had penetrated right through my coat and blue jeans. My feet, now that I wasn't focused on verbal fencing with Lisa, felt like blocks of ice. And a low-level shivering had hold of me. I didn't see the camellias or anything else. All I saw was the tree in the front room ready to receive decorations. And the boxes marked *Christmas Stuff* that I'd finally brought down from the attic, which had yet to be opened.

And not just the decorations. I also saw the faces of friends planning to join us for Christmas dinner, and Henny laughing as she had at Thanksgiving.

And Lisa was planning a surprise visit just before Christmas to drop this news on all of us?

How was I supposed to *not* tell Henny and the others? Could I go on for the next two weeks as if nothing had changed, to allow Lisa to break the news personally? Like most human beings, I could bend the truth when I needed to, but this felt outright deceitful—*lying to the person who depended on me and trusted me utterly.*

Merry Christmas to all of us at Hennipen House.

I hunched over, hugging myself, trying not to let the rising nausea take over. I rocked back and forth, wishing I could just give in, give up, and walk away.

Aunt Henny would be fine. It might be different for her. But Lisa was probably right. She would adjust, especially as her dementia worsened. She'd probably be happy enough, and maybe she'd be safer. But I knew it wasn't what the old Henny—the one I knew best—would've wanted. She would've risked everything—including her life—to stay here.

I pulled my phone back out of my pocket and called Mom, irate.

"You should've told me."

"Amelia? You don't sound like yourself. What's wrong?"

"I spoke to Lisa."

"Oh. What do you think of her plan?"

"It stinks, Mom. I thought we were all on the same page. We were keeping Henny at home as she'd asked. We promised. Including Lisa."

"She gave it a lot of thought. She's been through so much, Amelia, with the surgery and the chemo treatments. Reality is that she's doing better, but it was a wake-up call. She can't be certain of continuing to get better. And suppose Lisa can't . . . isn't able to follow through with making those decisions a year from now. She can't, in good conscience, leave it hanging, undealt with like this."

"Seriously? What's changed? Lisa was good with this until now."

"Because she can handle it now. She might not be

able to do this in the future. She'll get Henny settled in the new place, and then she'll be able to sell the house and property to cover expenses and—"

"Is that it? Oh, I can accept that maybe some of this is practical—I get that—but Lisa hates this place. She wants to liquidate it now."

"Okay. Yes, but the point is that she'll have to liquidate Henny's assets to cover expenses at the new facility and such."

Words deserted me.

"Amelia. Consider this logically. There's only one way that this is going to end for Henny. Lisa is trying to do the responsible, caring thing." She paused, then added, "Plus, it's time you took your life back, my darling. You deserve a life."

"That isn't for you to say, Mom. I've made my life. It isn't perfect. Sometimes I even resent it. But that's for me to decide. For now, Henny can afford the bills for the house and for her caregivers. Until Henny needs care that she can't receive here, then Lisa needs to . . . I don't know what, but she needs to *not* do this. Not yet."

The words that came from me were hoarse as I said, "And why would she do this a week or so before Christmas?"

Mom made a soft sound, like a sigh. "Well, she has commitments down here for Christmas so she needs to be back here for those."

I disconnected.

How was I going to face Henny, act as though we were on track for another dinner with friends at Hennipen

House? Apparently, her last holiday there.

ⱥ

I made it through late afternoon. When Megan asked what was wrong, I blamed a headache.

"Do you need me to stay until Bianca arrives? You look a little green. But I don't think Henny should be on her own, even for that short while. She's a little off too, after all the holiday fun."

"I'm fine. I'll hang in."

Megan left. Henny was already settled in watching television. I realized I'd never put her mama's silver back into the box. I'd wrapped the utensils up in a clean dish towel and left it and the tray just inside the small room, but I hadn't gotten around to stowing it away properly.

I decided to bring the box and utensils back to the kitchen. I could listen out for Henny while I put it all away neatly. Which I did, but when I went to put the box and tray in the sideboard drawer, I saw the manila envelope again. Saw my name on it along with Henny's and Simon's.

I pulled it out and carried it back to the kitchen. I checked on Henny. She'd dozed off in her chair. I returned to the kitchen and opened the folder.

Mr. Forester's card was paper-clipped to the document inside the envelope, along with a cover letter.

Was I supposed to vanish from Henny's life—as Simon had vanished from ours? It broke my heart to think of it.

With a sense of defeat, or perhaps simply farewell, I paged through the legal document. Then I frowned. I went back and read the cover letter, then started again with page one.

I set the document down on the table, confused. Almost afraid to think it through.

Tomorrow, I thought. *I'll consider it again tomorrow when things feel right side up again. When I'm stronger.*

Bianca arrived about nine. I told Henny good night and said I'd see her tomorrow.

"I have a few things to take care of in the morning, Henny, but when I come back over here tomorrow, no matter what, we're going to open those boxes of Christmas decorations. We're going to light up Hennipen House this Christmas." I leaned close, face-to-face. "Does that sound good to you?"

"Christmas," she echoed. Then she added, "Christmas is my favorite holiday."

"I don't doubt it a bit, Henny. Sleep well and rest up for tomorrow."

If this was going to be her last Christmas here, then we'd go all out and do it right.

And if it wasn't? Then all the more reason to celebrate.

⟡

When I left, it was dark out. It meant I'd be walking home by the light of a flashlight. Didn't matter. I'd been traveling on that path for so many years that I could've done it by moonlight alone.

I took one of the generic tote bags we had hanging in the laundry room and put the manila envelope in it—it was going with me and staying with me. And in the morning, I'd be making a call to Forester Jr.

Chapter Twelve

I had an appointment with Henny's attorney—rather, his son—Benjamin Forester Jr. I'd called just in the nick of time. He and his family were preparing to leave for a holiday trip. He agreed that if I could meet him at the office the next morning, we could discuss the situation.

The younger Mr. Forester looked nothing like his father. He was slim, mostly gray, but whether it was genetics or differences in health care or whatever, he looked fit and I saw no sign of arthritic fingers.

I apologized to him. "I'm sorry, but it was your father's hands that I mostly recall from that visit. He explained the document—the trust—but I don't remember much of what he said, except that on Henny's death Simon and I would receive the Hennipen property. But Simon left and then he died . . . the term is *predeceased*, right? He predeceased Henny."

Mr. Forester nodded.

"Can you explain what that means to me in terms of this document?"

He looked through it, checking dates and signatures, and seemed to give the body of it a swift, general once-over.

"There was a later, updated document," he said. "I

had my paralegal pull it before you came over."

A later document? My heart sank and lifted—both at the same time. *Crazy.* I was still divided about what I considered the best outcome. Lisa wasn't necessarily wrong in what she'd said. Neither was I. But Henny was the one who'd suffer or not, depending upon which one of us ended up being right—and as far as I could figure, only a fortune teller would try to guess which.

"So the summary is that my father was the trustee for this trust. When he was closing his practice, I was appointed the trustee. Henny approved. Legally, we didn't need her approval, but Father had great respect for her and for his long association with the Hennipen family. So that was the only change. The trust still stands and will do so until Mary Hennipen, known as Henny, is deceased or is ruled incompetent. At that time, the property will go to her grandson Simon and/or to her granddaughter-in-law, Amelia—you," Forester Jr. said.

"Mrs. Hennipen had the trust set up so that you both, or failing that, the survivor, becomes the owner of the house and land on her death or if she's declared incapacitated."

I was stunned. I couldn't speak.

Mr. Forester handed me a bottle of water. "Take a drink and breathe."

He watched me and seemed reassured by what he saw. "So you said you weren't listening to my father the day he explained it?"

"Simon and I had only been married five years. We were so young. I had no reason to think that he'd be gone so soon."

"Of course. Well, that's life and fate, right? Henny Hennipen didn't wait. She was certain about what she wanted to happen with the Hennipen property."

"But her family . . . her daughter, Lisa, believes the property is hers to do with as she wishes. She has both Henny's power of attorney and her medical power of attorney."

"Powers of attorney do not affect the trust. The trust is separate from the rest of the estate. This trust is simple and straightforward. The trustee is the only one who can change it. The trust doesn't dissolve until it's executed, and that won't be until Mrs. Hennipen dies or is declared incapacitated. Until then, it remains in force."

He went on to explain that the person holding the medical power of attorney could, for instance, make medical decisions, and the power of attorney would give them the ability to make decisions regarding a person's estate outside of the trust. But the trust was outside the reach of both those legal powers.

He added, "Something to keep in mind for the future is that an accounting firm handles the payment of the property taxes. Henny also set aside monies to pay the taxes, sufficient to last for a few years yet. You're welcome to discuss that directly with the accountant. When the trust is dissolved, managing the property will fall to you alone, and you'll need to either continue with them or find an alternative."

⊗

I sat in my car for a while after I left Mr. Forester's office. When I returned to Hennipen House, we were going to move forward with decorating the house—I was determined. I'd promised Henny. And myself. Yet I stayed there, parked in the lot.

I had to figure out what I was going to do about everything else, and how, and when. It felt as though I were fighting through fog in an unknown landscape.

Even the blue sky that had given me hope when I left the house that morning had turned overcast. The heavy clouds overhead mirrored my own mental state.

This was a big deal. I couldn't even begin to imagine getting into this legal stuff with Lisa.

I called Nathan and left a message: *"If the offer is still open, I'd like to talk to you. Call me when it's convenient for us to meet somewhere away from Hennipen House."*

⊗

Henny was napping when I reached Hennipen House, which was just as well because my poor brain was so scattered I didn't know up from down. It seemed like a good time to take a look inside the Christmas boxes that I'd left in the front room near the tree, but even though I was lifting flaps, nothing stuck in my brain. I was wasting time. I needed clear next steps.

Megan greeted me. When she saw my face, she frowned. "You're back, I see. What's up with you? You haven't been yourself for a few days now."

I pressed my lips together and shrugged.

"Amelia. You know you can talk to me. We've known each other for years now."

Impetuously, I gave her a quick hug. "I will when I can. There's something on my mind . . . I need it clearer in my head before I discuss it."

A truck pulled up outside. Nathan's.

Megan heard it too and went to the window, pushing aside the lace curtains. She looked back at me, her expression fierce. "This mood, whatever this is on your mind . . . It isn't his fault, is it?"

"No. Oh goodness, no."

"Promise?"

"Promise."

"Okay then."

He knocked.

"I want to speak with him. He's here because I asked him."

"Okay," she said again, and walked away. "Yell if you need me."

I watched her stride up the hallway, and I sighed—I was no good at deceit—then I remembered Nathan was waiting at the door.

When I opened the door, I paused. His face. His expression. Was that expectation or apprehension? Was he going to run as soon as he saw trouble was here? Trouble in the person of me?

"Can I talk to you about something?"

He hesitated. I could hardly blame him, considering the tension in my voice and likely the crazed look on my face.

"Sure?"

Yes, he said it as a question—unsure of that "sure."

Sound traveled up the wide hallway and along the high ceilings. I said, "Walk with me?"

"Okay." He sounded more certain this time.

"It's gotten cold out there." I stepped back. "Come in while I get my coat."

⌘

It was cold. The wind had picked up. I wanted to talk in private. I couldn't risk being overheard by the people I cared about inside that house. And I needed fresh air to breathe.

I took advantage of Nathan, putting my arm through his, borrowing some of his calm. His strength. I led him around the house and out back to the woods. To the red-ribboned tree and the evergreens. We were still relatively near the house, but far enough away, and hidden well enough, for a private conversation.

I looked at him and said, "I don't know where to begin."

The trees and bushes in the old garden blocked the worst of the wind, but it wasn't much shelter from the cold otherwise. Other than the bright spots of red provided by the bows on the sapling, it was drab out here. Drab everywhere.

Nathan stayed close. He said, "Begin wherever you want."

"At the beginning?" I said it sarcastically. "I don't even know where or what the beginning is."

"So, then, start at the end."

I smiled a little. "The end?" I nodded. "Okay, I spoke with an attorney this morning."

"Why?"

"About a trust. You know, a legal trust. Henny set one up years ago, back while Simon and I were married. I thought that when Simon died, the trust ended since he wouldn't be around to inherit, but I never gave it much thought. It never felt like a real thing anyway. Does that make sense?"

"Sure. Legal things seem pretty obscure to most of us."

"Yeah."

"So what brought it up now?"

I sighed and tried to stop the stinging in my eyes. If I cried out here, I'd get icicles on my lashes and cheeks— it was that cold. Nathan had taken my hands—I'd forgotten my gloves—and was holding them in his own.

"Henny's daughter, Lisa, wants to move her to Florida, but not to live with her. She wants to move her to a memory-care facility down there."

He waited.

"To a place she *doesn't* know, away from the people she *does* know—people she's known for years as her friends and caregivers."

"There is a certain reality to what's happening with Henny. Maybe it's not such a bad idea."

And that touched me somehow—hit me right in the darkest part of my heart—and I sagged a bit. Nathan put his arm around me.

"Come over to the bench," he said as he led me there.

When we'd settled on that cold bench, I asked, "Have you ever wanted to run away? Just run away from all the obligations, the things that didn't work out, that seem to tie you—chain you . . ." My voice shook.

"You'll have to speak up or move closer." He put his arm around my shoulders. "But I got the gist of what you said, and you know the answer is yes. I've been on my own, more or less, for most of my life. Practically since I was a kid. I made a life for myself. Not perfect, but one I fit into. Then my sister called and said she needed my help. I said, 'Sure, I'll come help.' But when I realized it wasn't going to end with her recovery and there was this little kid—helpless—who was going to be on my hands for at least the next twelve years . . ." He laughed softly. "See? I *do* know."

"Do you regret taking on Johnny's care?"

"Was there a choice?"

"Might've been for some people."

"He's a good kid. He needs me. No one ever really needed me before." He paused. "So, yeah, seems like I need *him* now."

His voice ended on a soft note. I'd leaned closer to

catch his words, and he tightened his arm.

"Thanks for the warmth," I said. Maybe I embarrassed us both with the statement. Safe in that bubble we'd created here on Simon's bench, I was able to say, "When Lisa told me her plans, there was a moment when I thought that I could be free. A moment where I . . . was . . . almost pleased." I shivered. "It shocked me."

I added, "I'm still shocked. I made the choice to stay here long ago when Henny and I became friends . . . more than friends. She was like my mother—a better mother than the one who bore me. A friend, a companion."

Nathan rested his cheek against my temple. "You're hard on yourself."

A cardinal alighted on the birdbath. The bit of water in the bowl was frozen solid, so he perched on the rim. He tilted his head to the side and looked at us, Nathan and me, before flying away.

"Simon and I used to sit here."

Nathan withdrew a fraction, straightening such that his cheek was no longer against my hair.

I hurried to say, "No, please don't pull away. Please, let me finish."

He stopped, though he didn't resume that closeness.

"Simon left us. Left me and Henny both. I'll never know why. But I didn't take on Henny's care out of some kind of guilt or even out of obligation. I did it because I loved her. I didn't truly understand until recently how hard that task could be. And it will get worse. Even aside from how I feel, what about Henny? Am I doing what's best for her? What—if she could express it—would she want for herself at this time of her life, if she'd known ahead and could've planned it?"

Nathan asked, "Kind of sounds like she did. Plan it, I mean."

Stunned, I couldn't respond right away.

He added, "What about you when she's gone? Either to Florida or death? You were thinking you'd be off the hook?"

"That sounds awful."

He shrugged, saying, "Actually, I know the answer."

"Please share."

"You've been doing this so long . . . and your heart is engaged. When Henny is gone, you'll have to live with whatever decisions you've made along the way." He shrugged, and with his arm around me and us sitting so close, I was included in that shrug. "Bottom line, we do our best, but in the end, we have to live with our choices. For good or ill. So do your best and then move forward. That's it."

"Thank you, Nathan."

"For what?"

I smiled, knowing he couldn't see it. "For lending me your warmth . . . and your wisdom." I put my head back against his arm. "I should be thanking those red ribbons on that tree over there."

"How so?"

"Well, I would never have met you without them."

In the sudden silence around us, a squirrel scampered overhead and a flake of snow landed on my nose. Nathan glanced up at the sky, at the snowflakes still falling. Then he leaned down, brushed the flake from my face with his lips—and kissed me.

Chapter Thirteen

My head was clearer now. As Nathan and I left the garden and walked slowly back, I acknowledged I still wasn't ready to speak with Lisa again yet, but I was closer to it.

He said, "You'll know when it's time."

I'd once thought Henny and I were the sort of people who went along doing our best until the day came when we had no choice but to stand our ground and make a decision.

The time was here. But now, the *standing firm* part only applied to me. Whatever I chose to do, I would be doing for both of us.

When Nathan and I returned to the house, Megan had sandwiches on the kitchen table. Henny was already seated there, but her hands were clasped in her lap, waiting. Megan insisted Nathan join us for lunch.

Megan said, "Henny spotted you two crossing the yard and is determined to have lunch with you, so that's what we are going to do."

"And then the tree," Henny said.

Nathan raised his eyebrows. "But Mrs. Hennipen, Johnny's not here. He'll be sad if we start decorating without him."

"Johnny," she echoed. "Yes, you're right . . ." She

frowned. "Excuse me, but what's your—"

"Nathan," he said politely.

She gave him a quick smile. "Nathan." She nodded. "Yes, we'll start as soon as Johnny gets here."

He said, "Now that sounds like a deal. He'll be home from school soon, and we'll come right back over."

⟡

I thought I had time to build up my confidence before making that call to Lisa, but fate stepped in, and while Henny was roaming around the cardboard boxes in the front room, trying to be patient until Nathan and Johnny returned, Lisa called *me*.

"Hold on just a moment, please." I went to Megan and gestured to her to keep an eye on Henny, then I went into the laundry room and closed the door firmly.

"Lisa, hello."

"You called. What's up?"

"I needed to speak with you before you and Mom come for your visit."

"What did you want to discuss? You haven't told Mother about my plans for her?"

"No, I haven't, and it's been very difficult not to. It feels dishonest, and I don't like that. But I have other information you need to know *before* you have that discussion with Henny." I reminded myself to keep my voice down, before I added, "I'm sorry that we must discuss this on the phone. I'd prefer face-to-face, Lisa, as you yourself would, I'm sure."

"I've made the decision, Amelia. I'm sorry this is more difficult for you than I anticipated, but it must be this way. I must see my mother settled safely while I can."

"I respect that, Lisa. Truly. But Henny and I have things under control now, and if or when that changes, we'll adjust accordingly."

"Amelia—"

I interrupted. "Again, I'm sorry to have to tell you this so bluntly, but I only just discovered that the trust Henny drew up years ago wasn't based on Simon surviving her. It was written such that either Simon or I were the beneficiaries of the trust."

The silence from Lisa's end was profound.

In the gap, I said, "I didn't realize it until I spoke with the attorney, who is also the trustee, a few days ago. I'll give you his name and number so that you can verify this for yourself."

The silence continued.

"If Henny passes, or if she's declared incapacitated, the house and the property come to me. Please understand, I never wanted to own Hennipen House or to be responsible for it. But whatever happens, I assure you that what Henny put in trust for Simon or me will be used for her benefit."

I waited again, pressing my hand against the smooth metal lid of the washer. I wished I could cool my face against it. Finally, I said, "Please speak to me, Lisa."

Lisa spoke. Her voice sounded brittle. "She's my mother. Ultimately, I am responsible for her and you cannot prevent me from bringing her to Florida with me."

I hated doing this. I disliked conflict, and even though Lisa and I had never been close, this . . . thing we were doing with Henny in the middle between us offended me. I drew in a deep breath, held it, then let it out slowly.

I said, "You are correct. As I understand it, I cannot stop you from moving her away from her home to a place where she knows no one. But when you do that, I will ask the court to officially declare her incapacitated and the trust will end and the Hennipen property will come to me. And stay with me." There it was. I'd said it. I'd played my last card. My heart pounded.

Now I was hearing noises from Lisa's end of the call. Finally, she said, "I don't know what to say. Do you have the least idea what you're getting into?"

"I hope so. The hardest part has been trying to manage this team and Henny's dementia with my hands tied behind my back, always having to second-guess what you want, and doing it through Mom. Let me handle Henny's affairs. We'll keep doing pretty much what we—Henny and I and her care team—have been doing for almost two years now."

"It can't last, Amelia."

"No. Nothing lasts, does it? But for now, Henny is fortunate to be able to afford private care here at her home. Henny *knows* where she is and *who* she is with because she sees us every day. At this very moment, she is eagerly waiting for me to join her so that she can decorate the house for Christmas. We—Henny and I—will live in the present and be as ready as we can be for the future."

I added, "If you want to contest the trust, please speak to my attorney." I paused, then added in a gentler voice, "If you'd still like to visit us before, during, or after Christmas, I hope you will. You will be welcome. Henny not only knows her home, but she also knows you've been sick. Because of the time that has passed, she might take a bit to recognize you, but if you're patient, she'll get there. Come see her while there's still time for both of you to be with each other—in person."

There was silence again, and I added, "As you say, it won't always be that way. Take advantage of the time you have now."

She disconnected. Abruptly. I could hardly blame her.

Toward the end of the call, I thought I'd heard movement in the kitchen. I tried to fix a better expression on my face in case someone was still out there. Then I twisted the doorknob and opened it.

Megan was there. "Sorry," she said. "I wasn't trying to eavesdrop."

"I understand. How much did you hear?"

"Enough."

I breathed and pressed my fingers against my temples. I really did have a headache. "I'll explain more later."

"Up to you," she said. Her lips moved, but she wasn't sure what to say.

"It will be okay, Megan."

"Was she really going to do that? Take her away?"

"Still might." I shook my head. "But I don't think

so."

"Good," Megan said. "And good for you."

I smiled. "Time will tell." I added, "*Only* time will tell whether I'm making the right choice or the wrong one. But I *do* have a choice. That's rarely the case in such situations."

Henny appeared in the doorway, her fists at her side, clenched. She wore her exasperation like a woman who was beyond patience. "They're here," she said. "We've been waiting for you forever."

"Well, then, I'd better get in there or you'll start decorating without me."

Henny mumbled, "We already have. Just come and see."

◌◌◌

Nathan had returned with Johnny while I was still hiding in the laundry room on the phone with Lisa. Henny dragged me from the kitchen, up the hallway, and through the foyer to the front room. Johnny was as quiet as ever, but anticipation and excitement lit his eyes as bright as the star that would soon be atop the tree.

Henny and Johnny had already been consulting about where best to hang this or that, and I joined in. Most of the ornaments ended up on the tree. A few found homes on the lamps. Nathan was up on the ladder in the foyer hanging the mistletoe he'd brought with him.

I found myself standing beside the drop-leaf table—

the one filled with photographs of the people who'd been in our lives and were now mostly absent from us. There was Simon. He was gone, and this time, I felt ready to let him go in peace.

I'd been holding on to him all these years and only now realized it, as I felt that knot ease and begin slipping away.

Only a few feet from me, Henny and Johnny were huddled on the sofa having a close, whispered conversation. Their backs were turned toward me, so I couldn't see the focus of their discussion until they moved.

They had the red bows, a collection of them, now in a pile on the seat cushion. I kept my mouth shut as Johnny began dividing them into two piles, and when he was done, they each took their ribbons and walked over to the tree.

Halfway down the ladder, Nathan had also noticed something brewing and he paused to watch, just as I was.

Henny went to the Christmas tree. She looked back at Johnny. "Where? Here?" He nodded, and they each began securing the ribbons to the tree, fitting them in between the usual ornaments.

I heard Henny saying in a singsong rhythm, almost like a nursery rhyme, "This one's for Mama, this one's for William, my husband, and this one's for Simon, who holds my heart."

Johnny asked, "Who is Simon?"

"Simon." Henny sighed as she spoke his name. "My grandson. He's gone now."

Johnny nodded and said, "Like my mom."

Henny said, "Then this bow is for her. We'll hang it

here."

The last bows hung, Henny and Johnny held hands, and Henny announced in a loud voice to anyone who might be listening, "We are ready for our snack."

Megan responded from the foyer, "It's waiting for you on the kitchen table."

"Good." Henny and Johnny walked away, following the hallway to the kitchen.

Megan came over to me and gave me a hug. Only the second one I'd ever had from her. Then she did the same to Nathan, who received it awkwardly, but his cheeks pinked up and he looked pleased.

"I'm on my way home," Megan said. "Amelia, are you good until Bianca arrives?"

"I am."

"I'll see you tomorrow."

"Tomorrow, Megan. And thank you."

The door closed behind her, and Nathan moved to stand beside me. "We did good today, I think."

I sighed and reached for his hand.

"You okay?" he asked.

"I'm well. Quite well, in fact." And if I did shed a tear . . . well, that was okay too, because it was a happy one.

Their snack eaten, Henny and Johnny had settled in the TV room to watch a show, and I tidied up the last bits of assorted decorations, much of it going back into the mostly empty boxes. I also tidied up the bows on the tree, touching each one and acknowledging the memories and the losses they represented.

Nathan carried the cardboard boxes upstairs, and when he returned to the front room, he invited me to join him in the foyer.

Walking slowly toward him, I kept my gaze on his, and when he put his arm around me, I didn't object.

His face close to mine, his cheek brushing my hair, he said softly, "The mistletoe came with certain guarantees from the nursery, but I'm not sure they were being on the up and up about it." He looked at me and then at the greenery hanging over our heads. He said, "I think we should test it."

We did. And I was happy to agree that the mistletoe worked just as advertised. Perhaps even better.

☙❧

Over the next few days, items showed up under the tree. Ideally, one wrapped the gift before it went under the tree, but the gift was the main thing, right? Wrapping could be optional?

"Aunt Henny," I asked as I picked up a ceramic shepherdess who waited beneath the tree for someone or something. "What's up with your shepherdess being under the tree?"

"For Bianca."

"The Lladró?" I asked.

"She's taking care of the baby lamb."

"Goats, I think."

"Them too." Henny seemed quite satisfied.

"And the Waterford crystal butter dish? Why is that under the tree?"

Henny had to think for a minute, then said, "Megan. She cooks. She can use it."

She stared, giving me a questioning look, as if my wits were a bit dim. "I went shopping, Meelya." Speaking slowly and clearly, she added, "For presents. For Christmas."

Okay. Apparently, she'd done her shopping at the local curio cabinet in the dayroom and the china cabinet in the dining room. I shrugged. These items were hers to give. I asked, "Shall I wrap them for you?"

"Yes, please," was her answer.

As I wrapped, the gift collection under the tree grew. I asked Megan to add more Christmas wrapping paper to the grocery list. A couple of gifts with Henny's name on them appeared under the tree, too. From the moment she first saw her name on a wrapped package, she checked regularly for more. Like a game, I thought, and one she was enjoying very much.

We were only a very few days from Christmas, and Nathan and Johnny were coming over for dinner. We had a special treat planned for Henny, though she didn't know about the treat yet. As soon as she heard Johnny was coming over, she began to fret.

"What's wrong, Henny?" Megan asked.

She was sitting at the kitchen table having lunch and had stopped eating. "The boy. No gift."

I overheard. "There's still time, Henny. It's not Christmas yet."

"Under the tree. No present." She struggled to her feet. Somehow her shoe was caught between the chairs, and she nearly fell.

I helped her free herself, but then she headed for the stairs.

The stairs were a big *no* for Henny and generally weren't a problem because they seemed to intimidate her.

I put a hand on her arm. "What do you need? Is there something I can go up and get for you?"

"Have to go up. The boy's room," she said, and tried to pull away from me.

"What do you need?"

"Johnny . . ."

"He's not up there, Henny." I deflated a bit. She was growing agitated, and now she was getting really confused. She'd been so steady lately. It broke my heart to realize she was about to lose ground again.

"Henny, come back into the kitchen with me. We'll have some cookies. You want your dessert, right?"

"No," she shouted. "Go." And she tried to yank her arm away. Her words were jumbled. The only ones I made out were *Johnny* and *gift*.

And then I understood—as clear as the crystal butter dish under the Christmas tree. I knew what Henny intended. I put my arm around her and leaned in very close. Softly, I said, "I understand. I'll go up the stairs with you. You must hold on to me and walk carefully, okay?"

She nodded, her eyes showing her frustration, which meant I might not be able to trust her to follow instructions.

"Don't worry, Henny. We can do this."

Together, we made our way slowly up the stairs. There was risk. There was always risk. It was the nature of life.

Megan called up from below. "Be careful. Do you need my help?"

Henny and I paused to rest for a moment, just over halfway up.

I yelled back, "Thanks, Megan. Henny and I are managing fine." I steeled myself to say the words: "Henny wants to go to Simon's old room. For a gift for Johnny." I tightened my arm behind her. "Am I right, Henny?"

"Yes. Right."

"How are your legs doing? Are you ready to continue going up?"

"Yes. Let's go, Meelya."

"Yes, ma'am."

We made it together. I heard Megan's steps behind us and accepted that she wanted to be there to help in case Henny couldn't make it, or in case I faltered once we'd made it to the second floor and to Simon's door.

The door was unlocked but the room probably hadn't been entered in years. It had been his childhood bedroom and had never been properly cleaned out—at least as far as I knew—since he'd last been here. Maybe longer.

Megan said, "Are you okay, Amelia?"

I nodded. "I'm good. It's okay."

I opened the door and allowed Henny to enter ahead of me, but then I waited to see what gift—what treasure that had once belonged to her beloved Simon—she had in mind for Johnny.

The room was full of objects that had been Simon's treasures. Slick posters were hung on the walls, models he'd patiently assembled were displayed on the bookshelves along with a few special baseball cards in protective cases, all mixed in with the actual books. I remembered this scene well. Dust lay heavily on everything, from the sports gear on the floor to the replica airplane hanging from the ceiling, and it seemed appropriate—obscuring what the eyes saw, as time often did with the memories we cherished.

Henny stood in the middle of the room, her hand raised and her index finger extended, pointing at the air as if that digit were key to her finding the object she'd come for. And she did find it. I knew before she'd even made it across the room to Simon's bookcase exactly what she was after.

She cradled the once-loved toy—old but solidly built and quite heavy. "Simon," she sighed. Then she held it out for Megan to take, her arms trembling slightly. "For Johnny."

"Yes, ma'am," Megan said, and she went ahead of us as Henny and I made a slower but safe descent side by side.

ᙅᙇ

Nathan and Johnny arrived late afternoon for dinner.

We planned to go out soon after we ate, and we needed it to be dark outside. I'd sent Megan home because she'd already stayed late.

"I can handle this meal. We'll eat in the kitchen. No problem."

Lasagna, already made and just needing to be heated up, plus rolls and salad. Even I could handle that.

The guys were bundled up. It was cold out there, and the moisture in the air made the cold more piercing.

"Are we still on for tonight?" Nathan asked me quietly.

"It's cold, but not too cold. We'll stay in the truck, right?"

He nodded. "Good, then. Johnny's excited."

Johnny was sitting on the floor in front of the tree at Henny's feet. She was seated in a chair I'd carried in from the dayroom. I hadn't had time to wrap his gift which would have been a significant challenge given its size and awkward shape, but we'd stuck a gift tag with his name on it. It was a black pickup truck with a trailer, complete with a chain for the hitch, and rubber tires. The truck was made of highly glossed metal and finely detailed.

Johnny spotted his name on the gift tag, and his eyes grew round.

Simon had loved that truck when he was a kid. His granddad, William, had given it to him on his ninth birthday—I was there and I remembered. This truck was a replica of the one William Hennipen, himself, owned. I was glad there was someone new to enjoy it. One day, when the opportunity arose, I'd share that tidbit of info with Johnny.

In fact, it might be a good idea to get a new sandbox set up. A nice one with plenty of room for trucks and such.

During dinner, Nathan mentioned (with a wink at me) that he'd seen some pretty good light displays around the neighborhood.

Henny seemed not to be listening. I'd warned Nathan that this expedition might end before it began.

Nathan thought it worth a try. So did I.

Johnny glanced back and forth between us. "Lights?"

Johnny's interest must've communicated itself to Henny because she was looking at us now.

I said, "Aunt Henny, did you ever go out in the evening during the Christmas season to see the lights?"

Her gaze shifted, her eyes almost darting back and forth between us.

"It's cold out there. You'd need your warm shoes, your coat and scarf, and gloves."

Before I was done speaking, Henny was on her feet. I said to Nathan, "I'll help her get ready and meet you at the door," and followed her down the hall to where she'd stopped.

When we met out front, Henny laughed as Nathan picked her up and settled her in the back seat of his pickup truck with Johnny. I wondered if the act reminded her of a long ago day when her William might have, himself, lifted her up into his own pickup for a ride somewhere. Today, I checked to make sure her seat belt was securely fastened. Then I climbed into the front passenger seat, joining

Nathan.

"Everyone ready?" Nathan called out.

Everyone said yes, and he started the music. "Silent Night" played as we drove away from Hennipen House. As we turned left onto Maple Street, the Christmas lights, colorful and twinkling, brightened the dark night all along the street.

"Look," said Henny, her fingers pressed to her lips.

"Cool," said Johnny.

Henny was smiling and humming to the music as I placed my hand on Nathan's arm.

"Thank you," I whispered.

Epilogue

*C*hristmas Eve

Red is the color of love, some say. More than mere romance, I think. More than duty. Love is . . . I'm not always sure exactly what it is. But if we're lucky, we know it when we find it.

Red is the color of the bows on the tree—the one that's half hidden in the garden outside in memory of what was, and the one inside Hennipen House for what we have now, in this present—which does *not* exclude the memories.

Red is the color of Christmas, along with white for snow, green for garland and mistletoe, and even gold for the bell Henny wears pinned to her sweater. She jingles wherever she walks—which has its advantages.

Mom and Lisa arrive at midday on Christmas Eve.

I had wondered if they'd make good on their promise and show up. For one thing, it is a long trip from Florida. Flying shortens the journey but has plenty of its own aggravations. But they did come, and Mom drove a rental car from the airport to Hennipen House. As they park out front, a light, fluffy snow begins to fall.

I watch from the parlor window as Mom and Lisa climb out of the car, lifting their faces to catch the swirling flakes. And smiling.

Nathan hurries out to help them with their bags.

Johnny stays with Henny in the foyer, the picture book about the Christmas story still in his hand. They'd been on the sofa talking their way through the illustrations of the stable and manger and the animals…that precious, blessed babe…all of it, but I'd given him a heads-up about our guests' imminent arrival, and he was prepared. He's with her now, holding her hand to keep her from trying to go out the front door.

I'd been working with Henny, explaining that Lisa is coming to visit, along with my mother. I explained that her daughter, Lisa, is older now, and because she's been sick she might not look exactly the same as Henny remembers. And each time, I finish our little talk by leaning close to her ear and speaking in a warm but earnest tone. "Listen to Lisa when she speaks. Hear her voice, and you'll recognize her. Then you'll know."

"Lisa's coming. From . . ."

"Florida. She's flying in an airplane to come visit you."

"Lisa."

"Remember to listen to her voice. You'll know her by her voice."

Thus, I suppose it is my fault that when Lisa and Mom come into the house and they see Henny and her new best friend holding hands below the mistletoe—Henny closes her eyes. Tightly.

Lisa already looks to be suffering from a combination of fatigue and who knows what kind of maelstrom of apprehension. She gazes at me questioningly. Mom does the same.

"Speak," I say.

Lisa does as I tell her, saying, "Hi, Mother, I've come to visit you."

Henny's face squinches up such that the wrinkles multiply.

I nod at Lisa and gesture to her to keep talking. Lisa says, "It's good to see you again, Mother. It's been too long. I've missed you."

"Lisa," Henny says.

"Lisa," Johnny echoes, releasing her hand.

Henny opens her eyes. "Lisa?" she repeats, and she reaches for her daughter.

"Yes, Mama, it's me." Lisa crosses the last few feet between them.

Then Henny goes shy on us. I'm not really surprised when she seems to hold back from Lisa's embrace. But then I am *very* surprised—which is silly of me because Henny is often surprising—as she says, clear as day, "Lisa, come here my child. I've missed you."

Lisa gathers her mother in her arms, resting her face against Henny's shoulder as if she is the one in need of comfort.

"It's okay," Henny says. "It's snack time."

The next little while is iffy. Henny's confidence

hasn't lasted, and she retreats into distraction via the cookies. I take Mom and Lisa both aside. "This is how it is now. Henny's world. She did remember you, and it may well happen again, but it won't last. If you can meet her as she is, in whatever place she's in at the time, she'll be less frustrated and . . ."

Lisa says, "I understand. I just experienced a moment I didn't think I'd ever have again. I won't squander this time, Amelia." She grips my sleeve to hold me there. "But what about you and your life?"

"You've seen her. She's happy. She feels safe. I'm content."

Lisa nods. "Then so be it. It will be on you—your choice. Maybe this is the best ending anyway. The one that was meant to happen."

"Not an ending. Just another day to enjoy before we move on to the next stage."

We are interrupted as Megan walks in. "Hope you don't mind that I brought the kiddos over to visit." Morgan and Bea follow her inside and Johnny whoops, and Henny does too, though somewhat more sedately, and they go to the TV room.

I say, "Megan very kindly offered to help me get the meal together tonight. A special Christmas Eve dinner to celebrate all of us being together." I add, "I'll take you two up to your rooms now if you'd like to rest or just acclimate."

Lisa doesn't answer. She is standing in front of the Christmas tree decorated with both store-bought and handmade ornaments and festooned with garland beads and of course the red bows.

She reaches out, staring at the bows. "Just like Grandmother's."

"Pardon?" I ask.

"Mother's mother." She smiles. "She put big red bows on all our gifts at Christmas. I'd forgotten. Mother did the same when I was little, but with smaller bows. More like these." She shakes her head. "I'm surprised that she remembered. I'd forgotten myself until just now."

And in a moment that was wholly unexpected, Lisa touches a finger to her lips and then presses that same finger to one of the red bows.

Had Henny remembered what her mother had done? Perhaps not with that degree of specificity, but . . . yes, the bows probably triggered a response of some sort in her.

It may be that the same applies to me. Perhaps I'd seen them too, back when we—Simon and I—were very little.

I'd used the bows outside . . . because I'd remembered something from so long ago? Not likely. But maybe.

It is certainly in remembrance. And really it comes down to the same thing, doesn't it? We are often surprised by what binds us and ties us together. Even if it is only a tiny red ribbon.

I feel eyes on me and turn. Mom is standing there under the mistletoe, smiling at me. I join her there, not knowing what to expect. She puts her hand on my shoulder and says, ever-so-softly, "I'm proud of you, Amelia."

ೞ

*C*hristmas Day

I sleep on the sofa in the TV room in case Aunt Henny wakes early, as she likely will. I want the tree lights shining in the early morning dark to greet her as she walks into the front room. Will she remember it's Christmas? Will her timeline shift, or a reset occur? I don't know. But if she forgets overnight, I'll do my best to be with her and meet her wherever she's at in her timeline, armed with colorful lights and Christmas music softly playing, and a gift she can give and one she can open.

And it will be not only the best Christmas possible, but also the best Christmas ever.

Red is the color of love in all its variations. More than duty or desire, love is . . . I'm not always sure what it is since it tends to get mixed up with the other colors of human experience, but if we're lucky, we know when we find the right mix—the perfect match—for our life. For our heart.

ೞ

Thank you for reading A CRIMSON HEART. I hope you enjoyed it!

Author's Note

Crimson Grove does not exist except in my imagination. Since most of my books are set in real locations like Emerald Isle, NC and along Cub Creek in Virginia, it seemed good to clarify that. If you wish to visit Crimson Grove, you'll need to do it within these pages.

As to the story itself: Even when authors write stories intended for readers' entertainment, those stories often connect to past events or memories that have proven difficult for us to resolve in our hearts. We write from our hearts. And our hearts are stubborn and loving, and hurting and caring, and don't care about logic and good sense.

Many of my regular readers know that my mom died a few years ago after a long struggle with Alzheimer's. We did our best for her, truly, and tried to honor her wishes— knowing she wanted to stay in her home. But we learned the truth of good intentions versus the reality of what we could and could not do, even in love.

That said, the types of dementia are not the same, and not all family circumstances are equal. In the end, we can only do our best.

Fiction allowed me to give this created character, Henny—and all the ladies and gentlemen I met in the memory care units during my mother's journey—the gift I could not give my mother during hers.

~ November 2025 ~ Grace Greene

About the Author

Grace Greene is known for her women's fiction novels that blend heartwarming narratives with compelling emotional depth. Grace combines her joy of storytelling with her beloved characters to write books exploring themes of love, loss, and personal growth that resonate deeply with readers.

Residing in Virginia and with strong ties to the Carolinas, Grace draws inspiration from her Southern roots for the scenic landscapes that serve as the settings for her novels. Her evocative descriptions of coastal settings, charming small towns, and forested countryside in the foothills of the Blue Ridge Mountains create vivid landscapes that invite readers into the heart of her stories.

Grace's favorite themes explore the power and resilience of the human spirit, the beauty of the world around us, the tragedy we experience, and our shared hope—the core of which she credits to God and her faith. She hopes readers will find in her novels a journey filled with heart, hope, and the magic of storytelling.

For more information about Grace and her novels, check out her website www.GraceGreene.com.

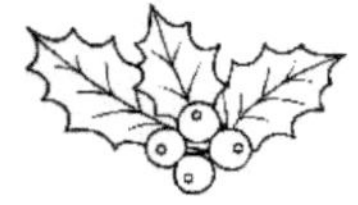

BOOKS BY GRACE GREENE

The Emerald Isle, NC Stories Series

Beach Rental (Book 1)
Beach Winds (Book 2)
Beach Wedding (Book 3)

The Barefoot Tides Series

A Barefoot Tide (Book 1)
A Dancing Tide (Book 2)

Single Title Emerald Isle, NC Novels

Beach Heart
Emerald Heart

Cub Creek Series

Cub Creek (Book 1)
Leaving Cub Creek (Book 2)

Single Title Novels in the Cub Creek Setting

The Happiness In Between
A Light Last Seen
The Memory of Butterflies
A Heart Beyond
A Crimson Heart

The Wildflower House Series

Wildflower Heart (Book 1)
Wildflower Hope (Book 2)
Wildflower Christmas (Book 3)
Wildflower Wedding (Book 4)

www.GraceGreene.com

www.ingramcontent.com/pod-product-compliance
Lightning Source LLC
Chambersburg PA
CBHW031540310726
48971CB00008B/2557